TINY GATEWAYS

THERESA HALVORSEN

NBBP

No Bad books Press, LLC

San Diego

ISBN Ebook: 978-1-955431-11-8

ISBN Paperback: 978-1-955431-12-5

To Brad, thanks for joining me in this crazy life.

CONTENTS

CHAPTER 1
RIDING THE "L"

A BIT OF MANURE, that warm smell of cows, grass, and farming, floated across the car of the "L" train, moving its way between the passengers sitting on hard benches. I looked at each person, their faces stuck in phones or iPads. No one wrinkled their noses. No one picked up their feet one at a time to look at the tread, looking for shit. Besides, where would they get manure in Chicago? Dog and human shit smelled totally different.

I inhaled, trying to focus on that bit of farmland, crops, plows, and horses. The stink of BO, pot, stale beer, and fake flowery scents tried to block me, but I pushed them away, closing my eyes. The manure smelled of friends, of home, of adventures I couldn't have here.

Then the smell was gone, like it had never been there. I hit my knee in frustration, startling the blue-haired girl next to me. She looked up from her paperback novel with a shirtless man on the cover and raised an eyebrow.

"Sorry," I said. I stood up and moved to the middle of the car, holding onto the strap over my head, letting the sway of the train move through my body. I closed my eyes and strained for the huff of a steam train that sounded nothing like the whoosh and thumps of the "L" careening through tunnels.

Someone's phone chimed, the sound like a train whistle. Had I gone through? If I opened my eyes, would I be home?

The "L" lurched and slowed, the bell dinging to signal a stop. I groaned under my breath and opened my eyes. Passengers shoved around me, trying to get off and onto the platform. I grabbed a seat on one of the hard benches, sipping the shitty coffee from my to-go cup. It wasn't going to happen, not today. Maybe not ever. Today I'd have to go to my shitty police detective job, and then take the shitty "L" back to my shitty apartment and stay in my shitty life.

The train lurched again as it got going, and a woman's high heel snapped under her weight. She yelped, her arms flaying, until she caught herself. No one moved to help. "Fucking shoe!" the woman cursed, taking it off and staring at the broken heel while standing on one foot. She looked around, obviously not wanting to put her bare toes down on the stains, dirt, and garbage around her. Holding the shoe in one hand, she clapped her hand over her purse, glaring at the person who bumped her. She was probably right. He was likely trying to grab her wallet, her keys, her phone, whatever he could grab while her shoe distracted her.

I looked away, the train picking up speed. The lights flickered, and I glanced back toward the woman. Her clothes changed, her face shadowed by a bonnet tied with a pink ribbon. I looked down, feeling my clothes shift, feeling the thin hoodie become rigid, turning into a corset, part bullet protection, part fashion.

Blink… a woman across from me wore a green gingham printed blouse.

Blink… a woman fanned herself with a feather fan, the tight curls around her face moving in the air.

Blink… two men in white starched shirts shared a kiss.

Perfume floated in the air, and I closed my eyes to focus.

Flowery and something the woman with the fan would say was from Paris or New York, but she'd bought at the general store in her local town.

The train began to rock back and forth rather than lurch and swish. Clacking and chuffs from the engine filled the air.

It was happening. A tear ran from my closed eyes, but I didn't open them. I didn't want to see my shitty world, didn't want to give it the chance to take back over. Heart pounding, I breathed deep. Unwashed bodies, alcohol-laced perfume, a fried chicken lunch, manure, and that smell of freshly plowed fields. The light in front of my eyes changed, brightening. I wasn't underground anymore.

I opened my eyes. A train car full of people swayed back and forth. The women wore skirts or thin leather pants, their tops covered by corsets. Some had gloves, some hats with feathers and beads, and some wore men's cowboy hats. Two women wore holsters at their waists, and you knew the rest had weapons stuffed down their cleavage or tucked into boots.

The men wore suspenders, high boots, tight pants, hats and, of course, guns at their waists. One had a curved French blade in a scabbard across his hip.

I sighed in relief, feeling my corset catch against my ribs. Glancing down, I saw my leather pants, knee-high boots, mud on the heels, and my leather overcoat.

Turning my head, I noted the man on my left; Deputy Johnson. My deputy. He turned his head to look at me, one eye a bright green, the other with a thick metal monocle over it, letting him see the surrounding magic.

"Sherriff," he told me with a nod.

"Lucy," I corrected him as I always did. I dabbed at my damp eyes with a handkerchief, pretending I'd gotten a bit of train dust in them.

Home. Finally, I was home. Hopefully forever.

A guy in a blue vest and black hat pulled open the sliding

door between the cars, letting in the train's hiss and dust clouds kicked up by the train's passage through the farmlands of middle America. He turned his back to close it and spun back around, a black bandana over his mouth and nose. "Everyone, hands up, this is a train robbery!" He pulled a weapon from his holster, and a red light pulsed as the chemicals within mixed, arming it.

And a train robbery in my first five minutes! Best day ever!

The passengers stirred as they grabbed their weapons or hid their valuables down cleavage or pants. I breathed out. If I didn't do this right, someone was going to die. Probably the robber. Honestly, why didn't they learn? The few valuables anyone would give him wouldn't make up for being shot.

I stood up, my coat billowing around me. Deputy Johnson armed his weapon, the whirring sound filling the train car.

"Aw, come on man, you don't want to do that," I said. "You're not going to get anything, and I'm gonna have to shoot you. But 'cuz I don't shoot to kill, you're just going to get hurt." Okay, in honesty, my aim wasn't that good, and I'd be lucky to hit him at all. "I'll shoot you in the arm or the leg," I continued. "You'll be in pain, some hack doctor will sew you up. Then it'll get infected, and you'll rot in jail waiting for trial. It's not worth it. Put the gun down."

I shifted, making sure the golden star pinned to my top was obvious. "I'm the Sheriff, and you're not going to rob these good people."

"Hey, Sheriff! Need any help?" The voice came from behind me, and I turned, my overcoat billowing around me. A woman with an eyepatch pointed a crossbow armed with bolts pulsing with various acids.

"Lady Amelia," I said with a grin.

"This is my train robbery," the man with the black bandana ground out. I really looked at him, at his balding head, skinny frame and filthy clothes. He was desperate.

"Drop your gun," I said. "There's three weapons on you. There's no point to this."

The man's finger twitched, and we dropped to the ground as his gun went off, spurting red chemicals onto the wall behind us. Someone let out a scream as the hot liquid landed on them.

"Take care of that," I told my deputy as I went to check on the injured passenger. I didn't even wince as Deputy Johnson's shotgun went off. The man with the bandana hit the ground.

"You fucking bitch," he screamed, though it wasn't like I'd been the one to shoot him.

"They're not bad," the injuried man said, dabbing at the pink drops on his neck. I poured water from my canteen onto them and gave him a handkerchief to hold onto the caustic burns until the train pulled into the station and he could see a doctor.

"She warned you," my deputy said, handcuffing the train robber. "And I barely nicked you." Deputy Johnson raised his voice over the other man's cursing. "Won't even need stitches. Just sit there 'til we're done with you."

"You had good timing," I said to Lady Amelia. Her blue-black hair was twisted partially up off her neck, tendrils everywhere. She pulled the eyepatch off. She'd told me once she couldn't aim without closing one eye, and the eyepatch looked better than her squint. Unlike the other women on the train, she wasn't wearing a hat with all the junk, but her corset had tiny red flowers on it, matching the tiny flowers on her green gloves. Her hiked up skirts showed three layers of colored petticoats, and her green-dyed shoes matched the entire outfit.

"Want some tea?" she asked, putting down the crossbow. "I've been riding these trains for days trying to catch you."

"I always come through the portal and find Deputy Johnson," I told her. "It's like I'm tied to him or something."

"I know. I've had to pay him to ride the trains up and down between Clearmesa and Pride Reach. I need your help with something."

"Anything," I said. She opened the door to a connecting train car and waved me through.

☾

I watched the steam drift upward from my china cup. Lady Amelia's servant, a large man in a tuxedo with a white bowtie, put a plate of cookies in the middle of the table and went to stand in front of the door leading to the other cars.

"Is it poisoned?" I asked. It was an old joke. I'd met Lady Amelia on my second night in this odd Wild West. She'd offered me tea, and I'd asked her if she was poisoning me. She'd laughed and offered to switch cups with me. I'd declined.

Then she'd hired me to find a fancy pin, a brooch, her husband had lost at the poker tables. Turned out the brooch was magic and gave the person wearing it good luck. It was worth a ton. Lady Amelia had kept the brooch, it winked at her neck today, and paid me with a giant emerald on a chain I wore now, the stone tucked into my corset. She was a liar, in her own way, but she'd immediately known I wasn't from this world. She'd taught me the rules of this world and somehow we'd become friends. One of my only friends in this world, or mine.

"When was the last time you set foot here?" she asked, sipping her tea.

"A few days ago." Eight to be exact. But I didn't want to think about my life in Chicago; the dirt of the streets, the despair, how the mold grew in the corners of my tiny apartment no matter how much I cleaned it. I didn't want to think about my microwaved meals and my days off spent watching trashy TV I didn't even care about. For a second, the smell of pepperoni filled my nose, and I held my breath.

Lady Amelia grabbed my hand. "Stay here," she said, interlocking her fingers with mine and digging her nails into my skin. "Focus on the feel of my hand, on the smell of the tea." She waved the cup under my nose.

Following her orders, I focused. After a minute, the pepperoni pizza smell faded, and she nodded at me. "Thank goodness. I needed you a few days ago; you took your time coming back."

"I have no control—"

"I know." She breathed out, putting down her teacup so hard the saucer cracked. "I just… my husband is divorcing me, which is fine. I caught him with a vampire whore in Silverbanks, so we're done."

Vampire whore? Magic existed in this world, along with strange metal machines that did the same things machines at home did, like let you see at night or shoot chemicals that burned like mace. But vampires were new. Were there ghosts and werewolves here too?

I couldn't wait to find out.

"I have all our money. My money," Amelia corrected. "He'll only get what he's stolen from me. But he took my daughter. And I need to find her. I need you." She flicked her green eyes up at me, normally mocking, but now sad. "I think I know where he's taken her, but I need someone to question the locals and get us where we need to go."

"You know my situation," I told her. "I may not stay."

"If you help me, I promise I'll figure out a way to keep you here. I have a few charms we can try. Talismans, if you will."

Her butler, or whatever, was on his feet, bringing her a small box. "I asked this woman from Cuba to create something." Lady Amelia pulled out a necklace with feathers, rocks, and a tiny mouse skull knotted on it. "Not sure if this will actually help, but can't hurt."

She stood up and placed it around my neck. Her fingers brushed my skin as she tied the threads together, and I had to work not to shiver, my heart leaping. She went back to her seat, and I picked up a shortbread cookie to hide my pounding heart.

"Thank you," I said, swallowing a sugary bite. "I'll help, but it's hard to find lost children. And I need to send Deputy Johnson back to Clearmesa. They can't be without a sheriff or a deputy for too long." Not for the first time, I wondered how I'd been elected Sheriff of a town I was never in. Maybe whatever had put me here had chosen a job similar to my police detective job. Or maybe Sheriffs were more like bounty hunters and private detectives here than back in Chicago.

"Once I found you, I figured I'd sent Johnson back. We're only half a day away from Clearmesa, and he's been keeping his eye on things." She pointed out a window. In the distance were small buildings and the haze of smoke from stove fires. The train blew its whistle and slowed. "We'll start asking questions here. I know my daughter and husband were in this town. We just need to find out where they went next."

My feet ached in my leather boots by the time we made it to the hotel where Lady Amelia had booked us rooms. We'd walked all over the town, talking to dozens of people—housewives bending over their vegetable gardens, kids playing with pig intestine balls lit up with magic-fueled lights, two bounty hunters who wanted to know what the bounty was for a missing child, and the pigeon master, responsible for sending out messages delivered by robotic pigeons. Detective work was the same, whether in this world or another; lots of dead-end questions, lots of shrugs, lots of lies, lots of things they'd forgotten or didn't realize they'd witnessed.

Lady Amelia had a description of her daughter, the likely clothes Betsy had been wearing, and a tiny image she'd commissioned an artist to draw of the girl for a locket. Many people said they'd seen a similar girl with her daddy, but we struggled to know whether it was Betsy or just some random child out with her father. I'd studied missing persons cases at my job in Chicago and knew the basics. I knew missing persons, especially children taken by a parent, were often gone forever. However, Lady Amelia's husband, Lord William, had almost no money. Traveling with a five-year-old, with only dirt roads linking towns every twenty miles or so, would be hard. Betsy wouldn't be able to ride for long, if at all, and the heat and dehydration would take its toll.

I'd asked the hard questions, not only of the townspeople, but also of Lady Amelia. Did Lord William love his daughter? Or had he kidnapped the child to hurt Lady Amelia? Surprisingly, instead of telling me what an asshole her husband was, how only she cared about their daughter, she'd taken a minute to seriously think about my question.

"He does love her," she'd said. "But what is a father to a five-year-old daughter? Yet he brought her a dolly from New York City. Very expensive, and she loves it. And he had a costume commissioned for the doll, complete with a little holster set and corset like I wear." She paused, lost in the past. "That was a pleasant moment," she'd whispered before straightening. "But not enough to make up for the gambling, whoring, or stealing my daughter."

"So she's safe?" I'd said.

"I hope so," Lady Amelia said.

I remembered how my mother had loved us too, but hated our father more. And my brother had paid the price with his own life.

Saying goodnight to Lady Amelia, I sat down on the

squeaky bed in the hotel. This place was dirtier than a one-star flop in Chicago. Mice droppings clumped together in one corner, and the room stank of body odor, stale liquor, and cigarettes. But it had a bright handmade quilt over the bed, and a pretty embroidered flower on the wall. I pulled a metal triangle from a pocket and set it up in a corner, pressing a trigger. Perfume, smelling like roses and lilies, filled the room, covering up the stink. It amazed me how many things in this world were like what I had back in Chicago.

For a second, the world wavered around me, and the light strobed, like we were going through a tunnel on the "L". Grasping onto the talisman Lady Amelia gave me, I focused on the feel of my tight leather pants, the pull of my corset, the smell of the roses and lilies.

"Please no," I whispered, breathing deeply, stroking the stitching in the quilt. I kept my feet on the ground, imagining them rooting me to this place. Eventually, the pulsing light stopped, and I opened my eyes. Once I was sure the world wouldn't fall apart, I stood, went to the window and opened the latch. I leaned out, inspecting the buildings. This was truly an Old West town, like what you'd see in the movies, with buildings made of wood and stone with simple names on the top: General Store, Tailor, Saloon, Hotel. I watched the people walk back and forth on the wooden sidewalks, odd things made of metal fixed to their faces, arms, and even legs.

A man passed by a woman, and she yelped, clutching at the missing purse he'd ripped off her wrist. She gave chase, lifting her skirts to pull a knife from a thigh sheath. A man in a black Stetson hat tripped the thief, causing the thief to fall into the street. A screech of metal sounded as the rider of a mechanical yanked on the reins so the thief wasn't trampled. The thief scrambled to his feet, only to run into this town's Sheriff, a tall woman dressed similarly to the way I was. Within thirty seconds, the Sheriff handed the purse back, discovered several more and perp-walked the thief to a building marked "Jail."

A knock sounded on my door, and I ignored it. I could stay here all night drinking in the scene below, smelling wood smoke, horse manure, spilled liquor, and clean farmland.

The knock sounded again, and Lady Amelia stepped in before I could call out an answer. "I brought you some clothes if you want them. I don't wear pants, but I've clean blouses and undergarments for you." Her male servant set several folded clothes on my bed. "I'd like to question those in the saloon now that the farmers are coming in," she said. "Finish freshening up and let's go."

Resisting the urge to roll my eyes because she was right, I washed my hands and face in the basin provided and joined her downstairs.

The saloon was unlike anything I'd encountered so far in this world. A robot, a mechanical they kept telling me, poured drinks from behind the bar, while two men dressed in black with shotguns stood guard. A pianist and a fiddler played dancing music, and a few men and women stomped their feet and rubbed up against each other on the dance floor, obviously drunk. Gamblers played poker and craps while drinking whiskey and cheap beer. Some men and women stood behind the gamblers, stroking shoulders, trying to get someone to take them upstairs. I saw one woman drape herself over an older gentleman, sneak a peek at his cards and signal with a wink to another player.

Lady Amelia bought drinks for everyone at the bar for information about Lord William and her daughter Betsy. Within ten minutes, we hit on the best information we'd had all day; Lord William had left town two mornings ago in a hired coach headed west for a town thirty miles away.

"Let's go," Lady Amelia turned to me. "We leave tonight."

"But we just got a hotel room," I protested. "I need some

sleep." No food or sleep would spin this adventure into a nightmare.

"I just hired a coach," Lady Amelia said. Apparently the man she'd spoken to had no problem taking the hefty bribe Lady Amelia offered him to give us a coach, along with his fastest horses. "You can sleep in it, if sleep is that important to you."

I tugged on her arm, her skin warm beneath my hand. "We're no good without sleep."

She spun to face me. "I will not let him keep taking my daughter further and further away." Her eyes were bright, her cheeks flushed with excitement and anger.

"Okay," I said, dropping my hand from my arm. "We'll leave tonight. Where's the coach?"

Fifteen minutes later, we greeted the coach driver, climbing into the squeaking box on wheels. Lady Amelia dismissed her man servant, sending him back to wherever her home was. She didn't speak to me, staring at the window, her gloved hands folded in her lap. I tried to find a comfortable place on the hard bench, pillowing my overcoat under my head to pad against the walls. We lurched, and I almost fell onto the floor as the coach bumped its way along the dirt road lit by blue lanterns.

It amazed me how our cars at home would hit a pothole and blow a tire, but out here on the dirt roads, the wheels made of metal, wood and a touch of magic always seemed to work.

I shifted and shifted again, trying to get comfortable enough to sleep as the moon shone through a hole in the top corner of the coach. It was the time of the night when it felt like morning won't come, and it'll forever be nighttime when I looked over at Lady Amelia.

She stared out the window, a tear running down her cheek. She wiped it on her shoulder. "We'll find her," I said, my voice loud over the creak of the coach. "I promise." I wanted to reach out a hand and touch hers, but instead twisted my fingers together. Maybe I was reading into something that wasn't there.

Lady Amelia looked over and swiped her cheeks again. "I hope so. Or he'll wipe me from her memory."

"Like with a spell? Or a… talisman?"

She smiled, just a quick flash of teeth in the moonlight. "Nothing so complex. All he would have to do is tell her nothing about me. Don't remind my little girl of the clothes I made for her dolly. Don't tell her of the times I sat next to her bed putting cooling cloths on her forehead when she had pneumonia. Don't tell her of the times I walked her back and forth and back and forth when she couldn't sleep at night. Don't tell her about the stories I'd tell her at night to help her sleep; the stories of fairies and magic. The stories of places where friends might appear from. She's only five. If he doesn't talk about me, I won't exist."

She breathed out. "It's the worst he can do to me, other than kill her, which he won't do."

"Once we find her, would you do the same to him? Not tell your daughter about him?"

She smirked. "It's tempting, but no. Not getting to see her again will be punishment enough for him. And girls that don't know the stories of their daddies don't grow up right. I'll tell her he loved her, but died. I'll tell her of the good times."

She touched my hand, just a quick touch. "Thank you." Then she leaned against the back of the coach and closed her eyes, though I was sure she didn't sleep. I watched her eyelashes flutter, her chest move with her breath, and her lips twitch until I closed my own eyes.

We pulled into the next town just as the sun rose, bathing the plains and basic wooden buildings with pink. The coach driver opened the creaking door, and we emerged into the cool dawn. I stretched the kinks from my back and hips and wrapped my overcoat tighter around me, trying to ward off the chill. This reminded me of overnight surveillances I'd done early in my police days when I cared about building my career.

The town was like every other, with wooden buildings and their names on top. Though this was a richer town than some; many of the buildings had two stories, and a few had brick walls. There were even rough planks over muddy puddles in the road, though I watched a rattlesnake disappear under one of them. I let out a shiver. This world was beautiful and challenging, but it had its dangers too.

Lady Amelia walked toward the hotel, the back of her skirts trailing in the dust, and opened the front door. There was no one there, and she banged the bell on the counter. I could hear the answering echo, like a doorbell deep in the backrooms where presumably the owners slept. When no one came out, Lady Amelia banged the chime again and again.

"Hang on," I told her. "It's six in the morning. Give the owner a chance to get out of bed."

Lady Amelia turned to glare at me, the shadows under her eyes showing her worry and exhaustion. "It doesn't do any good if they don't want to help you," I told her. "Be patient. Five more minutes won't change anything."

A door behind the counter opened, and an older woman slammed out, a black shawl wrapped around her nightdress and her hair in ribbons.

"What the hell are you doing? "We don't open until—" she began, but Lady Amelia placed a bag of coins on the counter. She held up the locket picture of her daughter demanding to know if the girl and her daddy were here, while I yawned. If Betsy wasn't here, maybe I could convince

Lady Amelia to get some breakfast, or at least some coffee. There had to be some bacon and eggs around, fresh and preservative free.

Suddenly, the smell of processed egg, cheese, fake meat, and grease filled my nose. I stumbled as someone bumped me from behind, and then more bodies pressed from the sides, like they were pushing past me, trying to get off and on the "L" before the doors closed.

Lady Amelia turned, grabbing for my hands, hers warm through her gloves.

"Concentrate on my voice," she said. "You are here. Feel the hardwood below your feet, the laces holding your corset against your body. Smell my perfume." She stuck her wrist under my nose. Lavender, dirt, and a hint of manure filled my senses.

"Touch your badge," she said. "Feel the metal under your fingers. Stay here. I'm not done with you, Miss Lucy."

The smell of the fast food breakfast went away, and the scent of tobacco, dusty fabrics and Lady Amelia's perfume took its place.

"Don't do that again," she snapped at me. "We're getting so close."

Before I could respond, she'd turned back to the hotel owner, asking her about her daughter again. The owner confessed that a little girl and her daddy had taken a room two nights ago. They'd bought a horse and supplies and rode out early yesterday morning, heading west.

"We're catching up," Lady Amelia said, striding to the coach. "Betsy was never good on a horse. She'll slow him down."

"We need a rest," I said. "A hot meal. A meal in general. We can't find her if we fall apart between towns. We should get some food and pillows and blankets for the coach. Just an hour," I told her, touching her hand. "You said you trust me. We need an hour."

It was closer to ninety minutes, and we had to wake up the general store owner and pay double the going rate for supplies, but it wasn't a waste. We needed fresh horses anyway, and the store owner had sold Lord William food, bedrolls and other supplies. He could tell us what the horses Lord William had bought looked like though, "two chestnuts" sounded like every other horse out there.

I should do some research on horses if I ever ended up back in Chicago. Spend some time preparing to make the most of this world.

"You were right," Lady Amelia said, about an hour into the drive to the next town. "We needed a break." She took a bite of an apple, her teeth crunching the fruit. "Thank you."

"You're welcome," I said.

She smiled softly and ran her fingers over mine. "I'm glad you're here," she said.

"Me too. But I still don't know how. Or why. Or why you know I come from a different world."

"My parent's house in New York has a library, and I spent hours reading there. There were stories of people from different worlds who came here, appeared and disappeared. You probably have the same."

I shook my head, but there were so many people in our world. Someone from this world appearing out of nowhere would likely end up homeless and then dead. No one would help them. There weren't Lady Amelia's in my world.

"So how do I stay here? What did your books say?"

Lady Amelia raised her eyebrows. "I was a child. I was more interested in the stories about knights in armor and queens holding court than stories of travelers. Once we find Betsy, I'll telegraph my brother and ask him to send me those books." She touched the necklace around my neck, and her fingers made me shiver. "But keep that on for now. Don't fade again! I need you too much."

When we stopped for the night, our driver lit a fire, and

we boiled coffee and ate dry biscuits and jerky. The memory of ordering food from some app to eat while sitting on the couch watching some ridiculous mockumentary felt like it'd happened to someone else. I didn't know who that woman had been, tired and depressed from her day, numbing herself on social media, whiskey, and stupid television.

I leaned back on my elbows, staring up at the stars, so many more than I could see in Chicago. I could usually find Orion's belt and Sirius, but only with the help of an app. Sometimes I could find Venus in the early dawns, but light pollution hid the others. Out here, I saw thousands of stars in shapes I didn't recognize. I searched for the Big Dipper, but either the stars here were different or there were too many stars to find it.

Coyotes yipped in the distance, and my heart thudded. I pulled my gun and thumbed the trigger.

"They found a kill," the driver told us. "But I wouldn't worry; I have my shotgun, and I'll keep the fire going all night."

I wasn't too worried, though I'd sleep with my gun next to me. I knew coyotes wouldn't bother us in the coach, and the driver wasn't stupid. He'd protect himself.

"Look. There's another fire." I pointed a little way into the plains where I could see orange and red flickers.

"It's a bit of a distance between towns," the driver said. "It'd be weird if there weren't any here. Most people have to stop to spend the night. There's two more out here," he said, pointing over his shoulder. Once I looked, I saw more glints of fires in the darkness. The coyotes yipped again. "Those travelers will have to keep their fires going all night," the driver said, spitting tobacco over his shoulder.

"It would be odd," I said, trying to find a comfortable place on the rock I sat on. "If Lord William and Betsy were out here, too. It'd be crazy if we'd caught up to them. If we were camping in the same place."

Lady Amelia stared into the flames for a minute, then stood up. "Ma'am," the coachman said. "You can't go walking into another's camp. You'll get shot."

"You comin'?" she asked me.

I stood up and armed my weapon, mixing the chemicals together. It gleamed red in the firelight. "They'll know we're coming."

"Good," she said.

The first fire we went to was a bunch of women with their horses tied up for the night. They offered us whiskey and luck when they heard Lady Amelia's story. The second camp threatened to shoot us, and I had to fire a warning shot in the air before they let us walk away.

The third fire was two people, one tiny.

"Mama," sounded in the darkness as the small shadow jumped and ran at us. Lady Amelia scooped her up, her corset creaking, and held the little girl close, kissing her cheeks and forehead.

Lord William threw a bit of wood into the fire, where it sparked up, but didn't stop the reunion. I turned my gun on him, but he didn't move. In the firelight he looked like an old man, his eyes sunken and deep lines around his mouth.

"You gonna fight back?" I asked him.

He shook his head. "All Betsy talked about was her mother. When was mama gonna meet us? What did I think mama was doing? Could I do her hair like her Mama's? Why hadn't I brought her dress that looked like Mama's? You won't believe me, but I was going to telegraph Amelia when I got to the next town. Tell her where we were."

He looked over at the mother and daughter where Betsy was explaining about all the horse riding she'd done, and how she'd almost stepped on a scorpion.

"I know when I've lost," he said.

"She'll make sure Betsy won't forget you. She promised me."

He shrugged. "Betsy's better with her mother, anyway. Daughters belong with their mothers. She should've gotten me a son." He looked at me. "I wouldn't have given him up."

It wasn't surprising Lady Amelia was done with Lord William. He was an asshole.

Lady Amelia strode away, her daughter tightly clasped in her arms. I looked back and forth between the two of them. Lord Wiliam sighed and threw another stick into the fire, the flames whooshing for a second as the wood caught. I should tell Lady Amelia to let Betsy say goodbye to her daddy. He looked away from them, picking up a tin cup and sipping from it.

He wasn't worth it.

Following them, Lord William behind us, I tripped over a rock I'd missed in the shadows. Stumbling, fighting to keep from falling, my foot hit a divot. Something moved in the darkness, hissing. I leapt away. But the rattler lunged, its fangs stabbing through my leather boot.

Suddenly the smell of pizza, cigarettes, and pot surrounded me. I closed my eyes tightly, trying to find that hint of farmland, feel the breeze on my cheek, hear even the rattle of the snake.

But it was too late. The doors of the "L" whooshed open, and people pushed their way past me, trying to get off and on the train. The blue-haired woman from the day before brushed by me, her paperback book clasped tightly against her chest. "Rough day?" she asked me. "You look funny."

"My foot hurts," I said. Someone screamed, and my body hit the dirty floor of the "L" as the doors closed.

CHAPTER 2
CANDLES, PENNIES, DANDELIONS AND WISHES

"HELLO! IS ANYONE THERE?" The man's shout coming from the shadowy forest was husky and the only voice I'd heard for hours.

I shaded my eyes against the glare of the Yellow Brick Road. Maybe I hadn't heard anything. Maybe I was hallucinating. Maybe I was going crazy.

Going? Asked my inner monologue.

Shut up, I told it for the umpteenth time.

A giant sigh trembled out of the forest, followed by the rustle of brush, like someone had kicked a rock. "Anyone, please?" The man's voice reminded me of my teenage nephew.

"Yes?" I called back. "I'm here?"

"Where?"

It wasn't like I had any idea where I was. "I'm on the…" I looked down. I'd been walking barefoot through a creepy forest on this yellow-brick road for at least an hour, and his voice was the first sound I'd heard, other than wind and birds. No airplanes, no cars, no people. I hadn't realized how noisy life in San Diego was until now.

"I'm on the Yellow-Brick Road," I shouted, knowing how ridiculous that sounded. "I'm here!"

I swear, if the guy in the forest was a Scarecrow looking for a brain, I was going to…

Tap your heels together three times? inquired the voice in my head.

Could you please stop talking?

Up ahead, a figure crashed through the trees and onto the road. He wore jeans and a plaid shirt, his skinny arms and legs flailing as he ran toward me. I froze, my heart pounding. This wasn't happening. There wasn't really a scarecrow running at me. I was having that breakdown my inner voice kept threatening me with.

When he got closer, I saw he was just a tall, skinny teenager about eighteen, acne still on his face. His too long hair flopped as he looped toward me. He wore a long sword belted around his waist, incongruous with his jeans and plaid shirt.

I breathed out. *See? I'm not crazy.*

The voice inside my head laughed.

"Hi," the teenager said with a small wave.

"Hi," I said back. What else was there to say? I was talking to a sword-wearing teenager while standing on a Yellow Brick Road in the middle of an unknown forest.

"I'm Dorothy," I finally said.

He raised his eyebrows. "And you're on a Yellow Brick Road?"

I threw out my arms. "Yep. What are the chances I'd wake up in a meadow two hours ago and find a Yellow Brick Road?"

He shrugged, glancing at the ground, back at me, and then back at the ground. "I'm Arthur, and I found Excalibur."

"Seriously? Like King Arthur's Excalibur?"

With a swish, he pulled the sword out of its scabbard and

offered it to me. Sure enough, carved on the silver blade was the word Excalibur. The sword was heavier than I thought; the hilt tarnished gold with a blue jewel on the pommel. It was simple and functional, exactly what a king in medieval times would use. I took a practice swing, nearly falling over. I passed it back.

"Like it was in a stone and everything?"

He nodded. "I woke up in that forest," he said with a shudder.

I knew what he meant. The forest was old, full of twisted dead trees, their trunks covered with lichen and moss. It wasn't the kind of forest you hike through to get away from the city. It was a forest monsters lived in.

"I wandered around for a bit and found a clearing. In the middle was a stone with the sword stuck in it. There was this shaft of sunlight, like in the movies. And… I pulled it out."

"Weird."

He found Excalibur, and your only response is weird?

I ignored the voice. "Do you know where we are?" I asked.

He shook his head, his eyes darting around to land anywhere but me. He needed to attend a seminar on eye contact. "I was walking from my class to my car and then, poof, I was here."

"I was at a bar with friends," I said. I didn't add that it had been my birthday and my "friends" were my employees taking me out to a stupid bar. "Same thing. Poof. Did you try your phone?"

"No service."

"Mine too." I wondered if my staff had even noticed I was gone or were relieved they could relax without their boss.

Arthur kicked at a rock on the path and watched it scuttle off into the woods. "Now what?"

"We keep walking until we find something," I said, wiping sweat off my forehead. "The road has to end somewhere."

"At the Emerald City, right?"

"Or Camelot."

We fell into step, turning a blind corner and almost colliding with a crouching woman examining the yellow bricks.

"Hello," Arthur said. "Did you wake up in the forest too? We did."

The woman stood. Her blonde hair fell in a thick braid down her back. At her waist was a plain sword, a jeweled dagger, and a gun in a holster. They looked out of place with her camouflage pants, black hoodie, and military boots. She'd slung a bright red backpack over her shoulders, stuffed full. Water bottles inside pockets glistened in the sun. My throat grew dry.

"Hello," she said back. Then she pulled her gun and pointed it at us.

Arthur and I raised our hands, like in the movies, and backed up.

"Whoa, whoa, whoa," Arthur said.

"Run for the—" I started.

Wait, commanded the voice. My feet stayed put.

"Who are you?" the woman demanded.

"I'm Dorothy, and this is Arthur," I said, my heart thudding. I fought to keep my knees straight.

You'll be fine. Don't be such a baby.

"Who are you?" I asked.

"Beth," the woman said, not putting down the gun. She looked us up and down, squinting slightly. "You're both human and not part of a story. How'd you get here? Did you eat a magic apple, fall down a well, buy some beans from a random storekeeper?"

Arthur and I exchanged a look.

"We both just… appeared?" Arthur offered.

"Did you come together or apart?"

"Apart," we chimed together.

"How'd you find each other? Did you just—"

"Hold it," I said, my arms shaking. "Can you please put the gun down?"

A frown pulled down Beth's lips. Her blue eyes twitched as she thought hard. I'd seen that look on staff when they'd been asked a question they didn't know how to answer. "Okay," she said, holstering her gun. "Let's go to the Library, and we'll figure this mess out."

"No way," I said. "I'm not going anywhere until you explain where we are and how we got here."

"Yeah," Arthur said. He put his hand on the hilt of his sword.

Beth's lips turned up in a slight smile. "Do you know how to use that? You don't even have it correctly. In fact—" She stopped, her head to the side.

"What?" I asked.

She put up a hand, like a kindergarten teacher. "Quiet."

I could barely hear… hoof beats? And metal jingling?

We moved so we could see around the corner. Four men on horseback in shiny armor chased a woman wearing blue pajamas. An arrow shot out and clattered to our feet.

"Into the woods," Beth commanded. "Go!"

I grabbed Arthur, and we ran into the forest, hiding behind a tree. My heart pounded, my breath wheezing in and out from fear.

"Don't go far," Beth said. "I won't look for you."

Gunshots rang out, so loud. I put my hands over my ears and peeked around the tree. She stood in the middle of the road, firing.

Why was she shooting at the knights? Why were they firing arrows at us? Why were they chasing a girl in blue pajamas? Where were we?

Beth cursed and re-holstered the gun after none of the knights fell. She pulled out her dagger and sword, holding one in each hand. The girl in blue pajamas, her dark hair a thick tangled mess, reached Beth.

Beth moved to stand in front of her, protecting her with her body.

"Should I go help?" Arthur asked.

Yes! The voice shouted. *Both of you!*

Are you crazy? I asked.

Tell the kid to use his sword. Then pick up a rock and go help.

"I guess, go help," I told Arthur. "You have a sword, at least."

He pulled it out and ran toward the road.

I picked up a rock. *This is a stupid idea,* I thought, creeping through the woods, hoping no one would see me. Partially hiding behind a tree, I threw. My first rock missed a knight by about ten feet and my second by twelve. I was getting worse, not better. This was ridiculous.

Arthur swung his sword, grazing one of the knights. He yelled a warrior cry.

"Get the girl into the woods," Beth shouted to me, fencing with another knight.

I ran across the yellow bricks, grabbing the pajama-wearing girl and tugging her beneath the trees. Suddenly, a giant firefly rose from her shoulder, spinning over heads while glitter landed everywhere.

"What the heck?" I exclaimed, jumping away from the girl. The giant glowing hummingbird... yellow bat... gigantic bird... flew at me, chiming like a text message.

"Tinkerbell!" the girl in pajamas shouted.

My legs collapsed, and I sat down in the leaves. A fairy. And not just any fairy. Tinkerbell.

"Are you okay?" the girl asked. I realized she was older than Arthur, in her mid-twenties, with golden skin. A bit of her pajama was wrapped around her head in a makeshift bandage.

Metal clashed on metal, and I didn't answer, looking back

toward the brick road. Arthur swung Excalibur wildly at a knight.

"That's not a fencing sword," Beth shouted. "It's a medieval sword. Hit with it! Use two arms."

Arthur clenched both hands around the hilt and charged, hitting the knight in the chest.

Tinkerbell flew in front of the woman, her hands on her hips, and chimed, sounding like a line of music.

"Whatever you think," the woman said. The fairy flew to the knight Arthur fought and jabbed at his eyes. The knight yelped, and Arthur hit him with his sword. Metal crunched, and the knight dropped to his knees. Arthur swung again, and the knight fell.

My ears rang in the silence. All the knights lay on the Yellow-Brick Road, blood pooling around them.

I was going to throw up.

You are not. Deep breaths.

"Come on out," Beth called. She flicked blood off her sword. "It's as safe as it can be in the Playground."

The other woman helped me to my feet with callused hands. I swallowed bile, and we both limped out on our bare feet. Tinkerbell landed on the woman's shoulder. The air reeked of blood.

"What do we do with the bodies?" I asked.

Beth hefted up her backpack from where she'd tossed it. "They'll disappear," she said, shrugging into the straps. "They're not characters from a story. They're pieces of an idea that just do the same thing over and over." She grimaced. "They'll disappear in a few minutes and reappear elsewhere alive. So you don't have to worry about killing someone," she said to a pale Arthur, the sword in his hands shaking madly with adrenaline. "Look."

Beth pulled up a visor, and we peered inside. A blank doll's face looked back. The woman in pajamas crouched and poked at the skin. "That's so weird," she muttered. "It's like plastic."

Birds began to sing; I hadn't even realized they'd stopped.

"Okay," Beth said. "So you're Dorothy, you're Arthur and you're…"

"Wendy."

"Naturally," I said.

"And somehow you have Tinkerbell," Beth said, ignoring me. I'd finally got a good look at the fairy. She looked like a small human with silver, glittering wings and red hair in a long ponytail. She wore a leather bralette and pants. Her tiny feet were bare.

Wendy twisted her fingers through her dark tangled hair. "So it's like this. I'm somehow in this forest, and I fell over a root and hit my head on a rock. And then suddenly I heard her. Tinkerbell. I know how stupid that sounds, but—" she shrugged and pointed at the fairy. "She got my head to stop bleeding and helped me find the road. Then the knights found us. We ran. And then we found you."

"How'd you get to the Playground?" Beth asked.

"I was taking out the trash," Wendy said. "And then I was in the forest."

"Poof," Arthur said.

Tinkerbell chimed. "She just appeared here," Wendy translated. "She doesn't know where Peter Pan is, but she doesn't think this is Neverland."

"Jesus-Christ," Beth muttered, rubbing her head. "And none of you did anything out of the ordinary? No deals with witches? No going through a doorway backwards, clicking your tongue? No finding a door that hadn't been there before?"

We all shook our heads.

"This is ridiculous," I said. "Where are we?"

"And how do we get home?" Wendy asked. "I gotta be at work in like fifteen minutes."

Beth snapped her fingers. "How does *Peter Pan* end for all of you? Does Peter die after drinking the poison?"

"What?" Arthur said, but Tinkerbell shot into the air, chiming like a broken bell in a windstorm, her glitter falling around us.

"No way," I said. "They go back to London with the kids. Right?" I asked. My fairytale knowledge was a little sparse.

"Tinkerbell drinks the poison. But she doesn't die," Wendy called after the fairy, who was high in the sky, glowing like a mini-sun. "Peter finds her and, to save her, asks the reader to clap their hands if they believe in fairies. It's a children's book, so naturally, that saves Tinkerbell."

Tinkerbell kept chiming, spinning over our heads. Arthur inspected the glitter gathering on his shoulders.

"But in my version, Captain Hook kidnapped the Darling kids and Lost Boys and made them his slaves," Beth said. "It's a terrible, terrible story, which means it's wrong."

"Nu-uh," Arthur said. "I just read the story to my little cousin. All the kids go back to London and grow up."

"You remember it differently because you were here when the Meddlers pulled Tinkerbell out of the story, and that inoculated you from them changing the story."

I felt like I was in New Employee Orientation. "What's a Meddler?" I asked. "And how do you change the story? Once it's written, it's written."

"Meddlers are the… bad guys," Beth said. "They destroy stories by going into them, taking important items like Excalibur away or even killing characters."

"Why?" I asked. "Why would that matter?"

"And how?" Wendy asked.

"Later," Beth said, opening up her backpack and pulling out a giant blue book. She tossed bottled waters at us. "We have to get Tinkerbell back into her story. You can come with me or stay here until another Scribbler finds you."

"Wait, what's a Scribbler?" I demanded. "This is making no sense."

"Wait, wait, wait," Arthur said. "We have to get Tinkerbell back into her story? How? Why?"

"Because every moment she's out of it is another moment *Peter Pan* isn't correct," Beth said. "And that destabilizes society. We need our fairytales to tell us right from wrong. If Tinkerbell doesn't sacrifice herself, children don't learn about self-sacrifice to help others. They become narcissists."

Hoof beats sounded in the distance.

"Hurry," Beth said. "The knights are coming back."

"Wait," I said. "Where are we going?" Why were so many of my questions not getting answered?

Suddenly, an erratic wind whipped around us, sending my dark hair into my face. I pushed it back just as Beth closed the blue book and stuffed it back into her backpack. A dark doorway leading to a moonlit forest full of dark trees had appeared in the middle of the road.

"We're going to Neverland," Beth said. "Or stay here. It doesn't matter. But I'd get off the road quickly if you're going to stay."

Tinkerbell flew down and settled on Wendy's shoulder. The fairy chimed twice, and Wendy shrugged. She stepped to the doorway.

"Wait for me," Beth said. She looked at Arthur and me. "Coming?"

Go with her, my inner voice whispered.

What if this isn't real? I asked.

What if it is?

Oh god, was I really going to do this? I was an executive at a Fortune 500 company, not someone who crossed into one world and then into another! I spent my days working, learning how to work better and be more efficient. I spent my evenings and weekends networking with other executives, thinking about work. All I did was work. I didn't have time for anything else.

I was definitely having a breakdown; none of this was real.

It couldn't be.

Arthur stepped to the doorway too. "Come on, Dorothy. It's an adventure."

Is your job the only thing you want to be? Because if so, you don't need me. And I would've left a long time ago if that was true.

I breathed out one breath and stepped through the doorway.

The passage was disorienting, like missing a step at the bottom of a staircase. But it only lasted a few seconds, and then we stood in another forest, one with dark twisted trees laced together to hide the stars over our heads. A full moon peeked through the branches, providing some light.

Tinkerbell chimed softly and flew into a hole in a giant tree. Her glow moved, disappearing and reappearing at various points. "That tree must be totally hollow," I whispered.

"It's the Lost Boys' tree," Wendy said. "It's where Peter Pan and the Lost Boys live. I can't believe I'm here."

Beth pressed her ear against the tree trunk. "I have to make sure Tinkerbell integrates back into the story." She climbed the trunk and balanced on a branch like a pirate walking along a ship railing. She cupped her hands around her eyes to look in a hole.

I shifted from foot to foot, trying to find a place where the forest floor didn't dig into my bare feet. "Think we might see Captain Hook?" Wendy whispered. "That would be so cool."

"I hope not," I said. "He'd probably kidnap us."

"Or what if we find Peter Pan?" Wendy whispered. "I used to sit at the window in my parents' house and look for the Second Star to the Right. I'd wish on a penny that Peter Pan would appear and take me to Neverland."

"I'd spend hours in the woods behind my Granny's house searching for Excalibur and wishing on dandelion after dandelion." Arthur said. "If I found the sword, I'd be a king, and no one could tell me what to do." His hands closed on the hilt of the sword at his waist.

"I wanted to go to Oz," I whispered, mostly to myself. "Every birthday it was my wish when I blew out the candles. I used to pack a bag of stuffed animals and hold it as I slept, so if I woke up in Oz, they wouldn't be left behind."

An acorn hit my shoulder. I looked up. Beth was miming something.

"What?" I stage whispered.

"She wants us to clap," Wendy said. "Tinkerbell must have drunk the poison."

We clapped until our hands were sore. Beth clapped too, peering in through the hole. She jumped down a moment later. "We're good," she said. "Tinkerbell sacrificed herself for Peter Pan, but survived, and that's what happened in the original story, right?"

"You got it," Wendy said.

"That's a much better ending," Beth said. "All about helping others, even if it hurts. I can see why the Meddlers went after it."

"But there's a lot of stories about sacrifice," I said. "Changing *Peter Pan* wouldn't change anything."

"But if those authors got the idea of sacrifice from reading *Peter Pan*, then there's fewer and fewer stories about helping others. It's a ripple effect," Beth said. "The Meddlers go into the stories and mess them up. They pick fairytales that teach us how to be human. And it destroys society. It's why everything is such a mess." Beth dug around in her backpack. "Let's get you back to the Library so you can talk to Myles. He explains things better than I do." She pulled the big blue book out, flipping it open again.

While Beth muttered, turning pages, Wendy looked up

into the tree. She sniffed and wiped away a tear. "What's wrong?" I asked.

"Tinkerbell didn't say goodbye. I thought she would. I've always wanted to meet her, and she didn't even care enough to say goodbye."

Arthur put his hand on her shoulder.

"Tinkerbell can't," Beth said, looking up from the book, her voice gentle. "She's part of the story again. She doesn't remember you."

"Oh." Wendy's shoulders dropped.

"I'm sorry," Beth said. "Truly. But you'll remember her for the rest of your life. And that helps."

She turned a page in the book. "Here," she muttered, pressing her palm onto the page. With a whoosh, a doorway opened, this time showing a room full of books. The wind whipped leaves around our ankles, and I pulled my blown hair out of my face.

"Jump through," Beth yelled.

Wendy looked around her, tilting her head back to stare at the Lost Boys Tree.

"Jump through," Beth said again, grabbing the other woman's arm.

With a shrug, I jumped into the doorway, Arthur and the others following behind.

When we landed, a man wearing jeans and a geeky T-shirt leapt out of his armchair, spilling coffee onto the rug.

"Beth," he said. "What the hell?"

We were in a handsome library, full of light and scented with candle wax and books. Comfortable armchairs and couches circled in the middle of the room, while the walls were full of bookshelves and books. I leaned back, staring up and up and up. The shelves must be thirty feet high and stacked completely full.

Beth dropped her backpack to the ground with a thud. "I found humans in the Playground."

"What? How'd they get there?" the man asked, throwing a napkin onto his spilled coffee.

"I have no idea. And this one had Tinkerbell with her," Beth said, pointing at Wendy.

"The fairy from *Peter Pan*?" He raised an eyebrow.

"Yep. We already returned her to the story, though. Peter Pan wasn't supposed to die. Surprise!"

"Guess that makes more sense," he said. "I was wondering what was going on. The books on the Modern Fairytale bookshelf shifted, but there weren't any approvals to be in those stories—"

"I know, I know," Beth said. "I'm going to get in trouble, but I couldn't wait for permission. The story had to be fixed."

"What? What happened to the story?"

"I'll explain later," she said, glancing at us. But I barely heard her. My phone vibrated in my pocket, as messages from the last ninety minutes suddenly caught up. I had over thirty texts. My CEO had started a group text thread to all the executives about an article he'd just read. They'd all had to comment on how awesome the article was and how amazing he was for reading it. Normally, I would've jumped in, making some important comment about some nuance I'd plucked from the article. But today, I tucked my phone back into my purse.

My life was pathetic. My inner voice sighed but didn't comment.

"We need some explanations," I said, folding my arms. "Because recapping the last hour and a half, knights clad in suits of armor have chased me, I've met TinkerBell, and still have her glitter in my hair. I left my shoes in some weird place where, when people die, they don't actually die, because they're not really people. I've walked a Yellow-Brick-Road. And this guy here," I stuck my thumb out at Arthur. "Has Excalibur belted around his waist. What. Is. Going. On?"

"Wow." The man blinked a few times. "That's a lot to happen. I'm Myles."

"Are you from a story? Like Tinkerbell?"

"Nothing like that," he said with a charming grin. I couldn't help but notice how handsome he was, with his green eyes, curly brown hair and slightly crooked glasses. "Characters can't survive in the Library. Have a seat," he said, indicating the circle of comfortable furniture. He put his fingers together like an executive about to give "constructive criticism," while we sat.

"The Playground where Beth found you," he started, "is a place where bits of unused story go. So if an author creates knights in armor, but cuts them from the ultimate story, they end up in the Playground, half-formed and without a character arc. The only way there is through a portal. Some of our books can create portals if they're keyed to you, but they're not the only way into stories. Which means you all went through a portal to get to the Playground."

Beth shook her head. "They said they didn't."

"So what were all of you doing exactly, before you got to the Playground?" Myles asked.

"It was my birthday, and I made a wish on a candle," I said.

"I made a wish too," Arthur started. "When I came out of my class, there was a dandelion."

Wendy smacked her palm against her head. "I was taking out trash before getting ready for work. I picked up a penny outside my door and made a wish."

"You all made wishes," Myles said, stroking his chin. "And the penny, dandelion, and candle formed the portals. Someone wanted you in the Playground and set you up."

"I'm more concerned about Tinkerbell," Beth said.

"Yes, good thing they found her," Myles said. "That was very lucky."

"It wasn't luck," Wendy said, with an eye roll. "It's like

this. What are the chances that I found Tinkerbell, Dorothy found the Yellow Brick Road and Arthur found Excalibur, all in the Playground?"

I stood up and went to the shelves. *The Wonderful Wizard of Oz* was missing, but I found a tiny book titled *Dorothy goes to Oz*. The other fourteen books weren't there, and the volume was much thinner than I remembered. Opening it up, I scanned the pages.

"According to this," I said. "Dorothy gets to Oz via a tornado, and her house lands on the Wicked Witch of the East, but she never leaves the Munchkins. This story is twenty pages long about her life with the Munchkins."

"Because there's no Yellow Brick Road," Arthur said. "If she doesn't walk the Yellow Brick Road—"

"She doesn't meet the other characters, get to the Emerald City, and eventually get home," I said. "I'm starting to understand. Where's *The Once and Future King*?"

Wendy and Arthur joined me until we found the thin book and confirmed Excalibur was wiped from the pages.

Myles frowned. "So somehow people who identified strongly with stories could get the Playground and remove items from them, simply by appearing in the Playground? I've never heard of that."

Beth shook her head. "The amount of spell work involved is impossible. The Meddlers don't have a Mage strong enough for that. We don't even have one."

"The Meddlers must have hired a new Mage. That's the only thing that makes sense," Myles said. "If the Meddlers figured out how humans can remove pieces of stories by being transported to the Playground, we're looking at cataclysmic chaos. The full and complete breakdown of society. No one will remember the original stories."

"Wait," Arthur said. "How do we still remember the original stories, but you guys didn't?"

"You weren't in this world anymore, you were in the Playground. It insulated you from the changes. The Library is also like that, though it's more in the real world than the Playground is," Beth said. "The Library is mostly in the real world. Your phone works, and you can pass through the door onto the street without a portal. But in the Library, we can remember the original stories if they change."

Myles continued with, "In this building, we keep all the original stories that teach us right from wrong. We create portals and protect the stories in here. Those are things we can't do outside on the street."

"So how did you remember the 'new' version of *Peter Pan*, if you've been in the Library? Shouldn't the Library have protected you from remembering the version where Peter Pan died?" I asked.

Beth grimaced. "We went out to Starbucks this morning, leaving the safety of the library. When we did that, our memories of the stories changed."

"Which we're not supposed to do for this reason," Myles said.

"I just wanted a Pumpkin Spiced Latte," Beth muttered.

"So, do we head to Oz or Camelot first?" I interrupted. "How do we get the Yellow Brick Road back into Oz? Grab a brick from the Playground?"

Myles shook his head. "We'll take care of it. Non-Scribblers aren't permitted in the stories. There's too much risk you'll mess them up. In fact, I would hypothesize—"

"We're not getting into that now," Beth interrupted. "Please give us Excalibur, and we'll get you all back to your lives."

"Wait," Arthur said. "We can't help?"

My heart dropped as something I didn't even realize I wanted was taken away. They wouldn't let me go to Oz. Tears pricked my eyes, and I blinked rapidly to clear them. I hadn't cried in years.

That's it? You're a vice-president at a Fortune 500 company. You're not going to use your leadership skills to fight to go to Oz?

I took a deep breath, re-centering myself.

"We're all experts in the stories we love." I stood up and paced, like when I was convincing the CEO of a new plan. "We might catch changes you would miss. Dorothy's silver slippers, instead of ruby, or Arthur's round table, for example."

Myles shook his head. "Trust me. We're experts too. You're hobby readers, not professionals. We know more about those books than you do."

I tried another tactic. "Could you let us go into those worlds, those stories, for just a moment? Without us, you'd never know the stories had changed. Surely, you can make an exception just this one time. We went to Neverland and nothing bad happened."

"Thousands of people want to set foot in their favorite worlds," Beth said. "These stories provide an escape for so many sad and hurting people. But the worlds don't like non-characters in them. That's why only Scribblers, who have gone through years of training and then months of prep-work are permitted into the stories."

"I understand," I said. I'd gotten my MBA because I was told I would never rise higher than a manager at my company without it. This was the same thing. "What do I need to become a Scribbler?"

Beth and Myles exchanged a look. Beth touched my arm, stopping my pacing and holding her eyes with mine. "Scribblers are born, not created. Our teachers start working with potential Scribblers in preschool. We're storytellers and misfits with voices in our heads. You aren't. We need to go into the stories to survive or we go mad. Wanting to go to another world just isn't enough."

"But—"

Not yet, said the voice. *I don't think this is quite your path.*

You just said —

Be patient. You've waited this long.

"You need to go home," Myles said. "And forget about all of this. We'll fix everything."

That night, after hours of plane travel–the Library had been in Chicago, of all places–I unlocked the door to my apartment in San Diego and kicked off the shoes Beth had given me. They were too small and pinched my toes. Myles and Beth had taken Excalibur from Arthur and turned us over to a secretary-like man, who booked us on flights to our hometowns. I'd said goodbye to Wendy and Arthur in the airport, all three of us looking like something had died within us.

I was exhausted, but still needed to prep for the Sunday brunch board meeting. Guess it was back to my normal life.

My eyes fell on my bookshelf with its beat-up copies of *The Wizard of Oz* and the fourteen sequels. My guess was Myles and Beth had fixed *The Wizard of Oz*, or the sequels wouldn't exist. I pulled the worn copies out, flipping through the dog-eared, dirty pages. Oz was a part of my childhood I hadn't thought about in so long.

I wiped a tear away and then another when they didn't stop. Standing in the middle of my ocean-view apartment, I wept. I'd give anything I had to see the Emerald City, just for a moment.

Be careful what you promise.

Wiping my eyes, I put the books back, showered, and grabbed my laptop. This was ridiculous. I was an adult, a vice president at a multi-billion-dollar company. I did not cry because I couldn't go to Oz, a place that didn't exist. It was Saturday night, and I had genuine work to do in the real world.

I headed around the corner to a coffee shop, hoping a shot of caffeine and a change of scenery would help me focus. Ordering coffee, I sat down at a table with my laptop, plugging my ears with earbuds and falling into a pattern of sipping coffee, reading and returning emails. The routine numbed me, pushing my inner voice and my wishes to the back of my mind.

The chair across from me at my table moved. I looked up with a polite smile at the nondescript man wearing the San Diego uniform of board shorts and a hoodie, his blonde hair lightened by the sun and surf.

"Dorothy?" he asked.

I took out my earbuds.

"Yes?"

"Dorothy, who walked a Yellow Brick Road?"

My face slid into a poker face perfected by years of office politics, though my heart thudded.

"That's an odd description," I said.

He sat down. "Wanna go to Oz?" He placed a book in front of me, a brown book, with a plain cover, its pages dog-eared. "I can get you there."

"But I thought…" I collected my thoughts. "I was told only certain people can walk through the stories."

"If we're careful, there's no actual concern."

I shook my head. "But couldn't the stories get messed up and cause world-wide complications?"

He sneered slightly, his blue eyes darkening. "Oh, please? Accidentally removing the Yellow Brick Road, which was a total mistake by an intern, by the way, caused our current political climate? Give me a break. We're not responsible for the degradation of society."

Outside on the street, a homeless man gibbered to himself, while pedestrians crossed the street to avoid him. I raised an eyebrow.

"That's unrelated," he said. "Social issues and walking into stories are two separate, unrelated topics. I promise."

I leaned back in my chair, taking a sip of my cold coffee. "So you're a Meddler?"

"That's a horrible name. We're Storytellers. My name's Liam. But what we call ourselves doesn't matter. I can get you into Oz. Isn't that what you want?"

I looked at the over seventy emails that had come in over the last twenty-four hours. Emails about plans to reach various metrics that changed nothing, emails asking for meetings, emails questioning the agenda of the board meeting tomorrow.

Emails that sucked away my soul. Sucked away who I actually was.

Ready to do the crazy thing?

"Yes. I want to go to Oz," I said. "What do I have to do?"

CHAPTER 3
THE CONTRARIES

I PASSED the baby to the mother, the umbilical cord still connecting the two humans together and wiped my bloody hands on a bit of cloth. The mother cooed, holding the baby against her bare chest as one of the other women helped the mother lay down, tugging a sheepskin blanket up and over. Other women cooed as well, the sound echoing the mother's. The baby blinked up at his mother, breathing easily as it adjusted to this world. Though my heart ached with loss every time I held a baby, I still enjoyed the peace of an easy birth, that moment of recognition when the two spirits of mother and baby greeted each other.

"You said boy," the mom said, her blue eyes boring into mine, begging me to tell her differently.

"I did. But he's healthy." I leaned over, rubbing the baby's back. He let out a soft mewl, giving a long, lazy blink as he stared up at me with the same blue eyes his mother had. "And a healthy boy is enough."

"I'm sorry," she said.

"Don't be." I touched her forehead, a blessing of my people. "There's nothing you could've done. Focus on your baby; he's hungry."

Within a few minutes, the mother birthed the placenta, and I placed it into a small bowl, passing it for burial to the teenager assisting me. I went into the room of the house where the family waited, a large room full of bright woven tapestries, functional wooden furniture and well lit by spell lanterns, casting a slightly green shade on everything. The smell of incense and the morning's baking overpowered the heady smell of the birthing room. "A healthy boy," I called out. "Mom and baby are doing well, and Queen Rhena and the court offer our blessings to this family and house."

There was that minute of silence, that minute of regret, that minute of hope dying, I'd seen over and over these last months. Then everyone remembered it was a baby, a reason to celebrate, and the congratulations began because a healthy baby, even a boy, was still a blessing.

A young man, presumably the father, ran into the bedroom to congratulate his wife and greet his baby. I went into the little corner with the washbasin and washed my hands thoroughly, finishing by pouring one of my sister's potions over them. The potion cleaned away the blood without reddening and roughing the skin, and she claimed it prevented infection. I washed my face, smoothed a few strands of red hair back into its braid and joined the family.

"Lady Lareida," said the matron of the house, her silvered hair held back from her face with a bit of patterned cloth. "Thank you for coming. The births are always easier with you and your skills present."

"It was an easy birth with a powerful mother; she did all the work. It was pure coincidence I was present and in the area," I lied. The matron inclined her head, possibly catching my lie. She ordered one of the children running around to get me some food, and I gratefully sank into a cushioned chair for a moment.

The queen, my sister, had ordered me to attend every birth possible within her kingdom of Punthyn. Some days, I assisted at two or three births, and sometimes I had a break for a day or two before the next summons came.

I scrubbed my hand over my face. I didn't need as much sleep as full-blooded humans, but I felt the pressure of the last few months. The strain of rubbing backs and feet, helping women into birthing positions, finally kneeling on the floor as they delivered the babies, wore on my body. And then there was the emotional pain when a baby wasn't born healthy. Or the labor was harder on the mother than expected. I hadn't lost anyone, but that was because our women were strong and healthy, rather than anything I did.

A memory of my daughter's birth floated through my mind, the first time I'd seen her dark hair, pale skin and such perfect pointed ears. She'd been barely more than a baby herself when a spider bite had taken her. I closed my eyes, willing the memory away. I was tired and reaching my mental and physical limits.

The family seemed to sense my exhaustion, and let me sit quietly, surrounded by the light and congratulations of the family. I stared, falling into the swirls of color on a tapestry depicting a gentle farm scene, my father's castle in the background. It reminded me I owed Queen Rhena an update.

I accepted a meat pie and a cup of home-brewed ale from a child, with gratitude, before stepping outside to speak to my sister. The night air was cool on my heated cheeks, and I walked a little way from the lighted cottages into the forest, enjoying the salty meat and bitter ale combination. The sky above shone with glittering stars, and the two moons lit my way, though I didn't need them to see in the forest.

I pulled a small black mirror from my pocket and swiped across the surface, pushing magic into the glass. After a minute, my sister's face, Queen Rhena, filled the glass. "Already?" she said. "That was fast. Is the baby healthy?" she asked, her attention half on a scroll in her hand.

"Yes, but it's another boy," I said, leaning against a trunk, the wood warm at my back, the leaves lit by tiny sparkles of light. "I think I've attended over seventy births in the last three months. All but three were boys."

"Seventy-eight," Rhena said. "Seventy-eight births. Seventy-five more boys." She sighed. Her hair was down, framing her face, her crown set aside, the bags beneath her eyes prevalent. It wasn't often I saw her looking her true age, with the worries of ruling our kingdom apparent across her face.

She needed to refresh her glamour.

"We should convene the council," I said. "Seventy-five more boys makes it clear. There won't be enough women; there's not now. In fifty years, we'll be inbred and unrecognizable. Without opening the Gateway or trading with another kingdom, your reign will fall. Our people will fall."

"Either possibility is unacceptable. I need a different solution."

I bit my lip. Arguing with Rhena had to be done carefully, and I was tired. "There isn't one. We either open the Gateway, allowing Contraries through, allowing them to mingle with our people, or we allow the other kingdoms past our walls. Perhaps we invite the other kingdoms to a festival. Offer trade. Offer to exchange children or families. Or perhaps we take on fifty of their girls. Orphans and the like. It would take time, but eventually our children would come together, solving our problem."

"I won't trade with the other kingdoms. They commit atrocity after atrocity on their people and their neighbors. That king in Mirfield had his witch put poison in one of their village wells. It ate the people from the inside. Besides, our kingdom has prospered since Father's death."

She was right. Like the other kings, Father had been a warlord. He enjoyed war, battles, and conquering other kingdoms, one village at a time. But under Queen Rhena, we hadn't fought a battle in over eighty years. She'd used the might of her army, the depth of our coffers and the strength of the lords within our kingdom to create a massive wall around her people. She and her council had declared we were neutral and refused to participate in any battles or even voice opinions on what went on in the neighboring kingdoms. It had been hard to ignore pleas for help, but the other kingdoms soon learned not to ask and now pretended we didn't exist, refusing to even trade with us.

But it worked. Our people ate well and were happy and healthy. They'd prospered with arts and literature taking the place of battle preparations. But perhaps our retreat from the other kingdoms had caused our decrease in female births. Maybe our separation had been a mistake.

"Then we need to open the Gateway," I told her.

Rhena sighed again, a puff that fogged up the mirror on her side. "We can't. The old council members won't permit it. The Contraries killed Father!"

"That was an accident. And we both know your kingdom is better without him."

"Lord Saynor would disagree."

"He doesn't speak for all of us. Either choice is poor, but we're out of options. We need girls. And I'm sure there are women who need a home, a healthy kingdom free of war to live in."

Her lips drew down in defeat. "I'll call the council."

"Thank you, Highness," I said, bowing slightly.

She smiled at me, just a touch. "Did you talk to your sister before contacting me?"

I shook my head. "I haven't spoken to her in days."

"Interesting. She was just in here, demanding I open the Gateway. That the Contraries are the only way to save our people."

"You made us your primary advisors; Kara and I often reach the same conclusions."

"You're both a pain in my ass."

I raised my eyebrow at the Contraries' language. The Contraries and their idiosyncrasies must be on her mind. Rhena wasn't usually so vulgar.

"Will you be back by morning?" she asked.

"I'm in the forest now. I'll be back in the Capital in a few hours."

"Safe travels, Lady Lareida," she said before her image disappeared. I tucked the mirror into my travel bag and pressed my hand against the tree's trunk. I breathed out, feeling for the deep veins and capillaries within the tree, reaching for the roots not only of the tree, but of the fungus beneath controlling the entire forest, controlled by the Elfin Heart. Invoking a spell, I breathed out and stepped through the trunk.

Daylight came too early. Which made no sense because I'd drawn the shades around my bed when I'd gone to sleep. The room shouldn't be so bright against my closed eyes.

I cracked an eyelid and winced.

"Did I wake you?" Kara asked. She sat on my bed, leaning so close I felt a puff of her breath across my cheek.

"For Goddess sake, yes! Get off my bed!" I kicked at her, but she refused to budge. I rolled over, pretending she wasn't there. "Go away!"

"But it's a festival," she said in a child-like voice. I threw a pillow at her, and she batted it away, laughing. "You were so mad when I did that."

"I hadn't slept in a week," I told her. "You woke me up right after I'd fallen asleep."

"I was just excited to see my big sister." She peered at me. "But you look worse now than you did then." She held out a cup of steaming liquid. "Made you something to help."

Kara was the master potion maker for the court, and her

potions could cure a cancerous growth, clean blood off hands, or allow the recipient to smell delightful to the person of their choice. But there were often side effects she didn't know about until too late.

I sniffed the liquid in the clay mug. It smelled of cinnamon, sage, and sugar. "This one won't keep me awake for an entire month, will it?"

"I could make you one that did. I just used one; it was great. I got so much done. Though I did have to sleep for twenty-four hours straight. That part wasn't fun."

I sipped the drink. The liquid rolled down my throat and into my stomach, warming and filling, the sweet and bitter perfectly balanced. I hadn't realized how tired and cold I was until the liquid filled the empty space. I drank again and looked around my room. It hadn't changed in years. There were the same green tapestries on the wall, mimicking trees, branches, and various forms of forest life. There were the same dark wood furnishings, the same view of the courtyard out on the balcony.

Maybe it was time to remodel. I swallowed Kara's drink again. "This potion is amazing," I said.

"I picked your favorite flavors because you're my favorite sister. Don't worry about the hours it takes in my lab to make every drop."

"Liar."

She flicked her white-blonde hair over her shoulder. "It takes time. But you're worth it." She clapped her hands. "Get out of bed," she ordered. "Take a bath, get dressed. I brought food too. The Highness," she sneered this last bit, "has ordered the council to meet."

"You know why," I said, finishing the tiny drink and feeling better than I had in months. Then I had when we'd realized how many boys versus girls were being born. "There's been three girl babies in three months. We need to open the Gateway–Rhena will never let us open up trade with the other kingdoms."

Kara grimaced. "I know. But I like the Contraries," she said. "They give us toys." She pulled a yellow box from a pocket and flicked it open.

"I can't believe you still have that," I said. "That's nearly a hundred years old." I shook the wax colors out into my hand and looked at the points. "You've been coloring."

"Not in years," she said. "I think the last person to use it was–" She halted. I remembered Ivo, my daughter, laying on her stomach, propped on her elbows, coloring on a random scroll. Kara hadn't been much older and had taught my daughter how to use the sides of the crayons to create lighter, thinner shades.

Kara's eyes met mine, and she looked away quickly, stuffing the crayons back into her pocket. "Come on. Get up. Let's go have a fight with Queen Rhena."

"It won't be that bad," I said, throwing back the covers and trying to pretend the last few moments hadn't happened. I sniffed dramatically at my nightclothes. God, I smelled terrible. Kara's nose wrinkled and, with a wave of her hand and her magic, turned on the water in my private tub.

"Bathe," she said. "I'll see you in an hour."

◌

Normally one of Kara's potions, a hot bath and a change of clothes would've recharged me, but not today. The last ninety days, and the fear I felt for my sister's kingdom wore on my heart and soul.

My maid, Lizabeth, helped me into a formal court dress, lacing up the sides and bodice with gold and silver ribbons. I wore the blue of my mother's people, which contrasted well with my red hair. Lizabeth used a wand to curl my hair, so it hid my pointed ears. I was the oldest of my sisters by about forty years, the result of my elfin mother being caught by my human father during The Hunt. Though the oldest, I was half-blooded and ineligible for the human crown.

I added a silver crown studded with sapphires, to show my station as the Queen's relation and advisor, dismissed Lizabeth, and left my chambers. I walked through the castle; the walls made of dark stone, tapestries and carved paneling, lighting the starkness of the walls. Gone were the weapons, the shields, and even the animal heads father had decorated with.

Rhena's council chamber was a circular room with a large rectangular table in the middle, comfortable seats pulled up to it. Rhena sat at the head, her thick dark hair twisted into a traditional knot with the golden crown of her station weaved within the twists. She wore her usual glamour of a young elegant woman, her skin free of wrinkles and her hair shiny.

I bowed deeply to her before taking my seat on her right. Kara, already seated, winked at me from her seat on the left. She extinguished the ball of flames she'd been rolling across her knuckles.

"You look worn." Queen Rhena said. "I think we've learned what we can and there's no need to attend so many births, unless you wish it."

I inclined my head. "I would appreciate a break."

"Then you shall have it," she said. "Before we begin, I just want to confirm that you both wish to open the Gateway over opening trade with another kingdom?"

"Confirmed," I said. "The Contraries were easier to work with than the other kingdoms."

"Agreed," Kara said. "I heard the king of Mirfield killed his own people just for sport. We don't want to trade with them."

Rhena nodded. "Then this will be interesting. Let's open the doors." Kara and I stood as the other council members, many of whom had served our father, entered. Standing in front of our seats, we waited until all entered and were in place before bowing, as one, to our Queen.

"Be seated," she said. There was the normal scrape of wood across stone and the murmurs as drinks were poured.

"Thank you for all coming to this council meeting," Rhena started. "I have some concerning news. Over the last three months, Lady Lareida has attended almost 80 births, mostly boys. Within a few years, we will not have enough girls to produce children."

"And it would put a tremendous strain on the women we do have," Kara added. "Our entire kingdom would shift to women producing babies. And even with that, we'll be inbred within a few generations. We need more women."

I explained the two choices: open trade with the other kingdoms or open the Gateway. I reminded the council of the Contrary benefits, how they'd created their own villages within Punthyn, intermingling with our people before we'd forced them back through the Gateway. I reminded them we had electricity via windmills to heat and provide light to our villages who didn't have a spell user. We'd received knowledge on creating wheels for our carriages out of rubber that provide better transportation than our wooden and metal wheels. Lady Kara's team of potion brewers benefited tremendously from the Contraries' knowledge of medications and ingredients we didn't have in our world. We had crops such as strawberries and snap peas we hadn't had before the Contraries brought them with them.

"While all that is well and good, and I appreciate Lady Larieda's analysis," Lord Saynor said, rising, his cloak swishing around his skinny body. "I disagree with opening the Gateway. The Contraries diluted our magical abilities, forcing us to rely on the electricity you love. Before the Contraries, not only did we not have a shortage of girls, we didn't have a shortage of spell users."

Kara scoffed. "We no longer have a shortage of spell users."

"Because we closed the Gateway," he said, wagging his finger at her.

"We closed the Gateway a hundred years ago," I said. "Forty years ago, we noticed the lack of girls in our children. It can't be a coincidence."

"Nor can the increase in spell users," Lord Saynor said. "But we can debate this all day. Are we forgetting the Contraries killed our king? In his memory, I'm not sure I can justify opening it."

"But it wasn't intentional." Kara said, putting her hands on the table and pushing up to stand. "Father's death was an accident. What happened to Father is the same as what happens to some children when they get stung by a bee. He was allergic to the food they offered. There was no way of knowing the big insects soaked in butter would kill."

On a holiday in their world, the Contraries had brought with them a bucket of odd creatures from their waters–large, multi-legged and with a hard shell. The Contraries had showed us how to boil the creatures still in their shells, in spices and butter, then bite off the heads and suck out the insides, the meat. It had taken us most of the day, and having to drink several ales to work up the courage to try it. I remembered the meat was mild-tasting, but the seasoning had been fiery and pleasant.

Father had been the last to try, finally unable to resist the idea of biting something's head off. But a few minutes after swallowing the meat, he coughed, then wheezed, and eventually stopped breathing. Our healers had descended on him, chanting over his body and trying to pour potions down his throat.

But he'd died all the same.

Our guards, their weapons sparking magic, had surrounded the Contraries, the treats the Contraries had brought trampled into the ground. The day could've ended with all the Contraries murdered, but the Contrary in charge of the Gateway on their side, Lord Sebastian, acted quickly. He apologized and requested permission to take his people back through the Gateway.

Rhena, all of fifteen years old, agreed, overruling the council members, including Lord Saynor who wanted the Contraries punished. She'd ordered the Contraries back into their world, forcing them to leave their villages and homes on our side of the gate. Then she ordered the Gateway closed, closed it stayed.

I looked around the room, meeting the eyes of the council members, the men and women who guided my sister with her decisions, who helped her decide what was best for our people. "Please," I said. "Father died a hundred years ago with an accident. It's not worth sacrificing our people. Three girls, seventy-five boys. We won't survive without diverse bloodlines. It's this or we open up trade with the other kingdoms."

"No," Rhena said. "That will open us up to war. And I won't do that to our people again."

"I call for a vote," Kara said.

"Seconded," Lor Synor said.

The council vote was tight, and I cast the final and necessary vote to open the Gateway. Lord Saynor couldn't contain his fury and stormed from the room, taking those that opposed the vote with him.

Ignoring his exit, Rhena dismissed the council, thanking them for their advice, and heading into her chambers behind the council room. She refused to speak to either of us, but we knew better than to take offense.

Later that evening, Kara and I sat on my balcony watching the mobilization of the army, supplies, tents, food and weapons be loaded onto wagons. Rhena had ordered over 500 guards and serviceman ready for the Gateway, an excessive amount, but perhaps it would placate Lord Saynor.

Kara handed me a glass of wine. "We need to tell the Contraries we're reopening the Gateway," she said. "Otherwise it's going to be a shock to them. Perhaps we should send a scroll through."

"Let's talk to Rhena. I could go in advance," I said. "Using the forest, I'd be back in an hour. I just need instructions on how to open the Gateway."

"I'll compose a letter," Kara said, taking a big gulp of her wine. "And I'll show you how to open it enough to throw a scroll through."

A horrible thought occurred to me. "What if that Lord in charge, Sebastian, is dead?" I asked. "It's been a hundred years, and the Contraries don't live as long as we do." Sebastian had been charming and intelligent, often staying for weeks in some of the Contrary villages. The Gateway opened in his home, and he'd recruited many of the Contraries to step through, coordinating the trade between our two worlds.

Kara frowned. "I hadn't thought of that. Did he have children? Maybe they'll want to keep the Gateway open."

"Perhaps," I said. "Or this could all be a waste of time."

☙

A week later, I stepped out of the forest closest to the Gateway. The army and their tents were spread as far as I could see; Rhena's green and gold tent above the rest. I crossed the field, trampled by hundreds of boots, to join my sisters.

Rhena wore her highest crown, a breastplate covering her red dress, and a sword belted around her waist. Her skin glowed, her dark hair soaking in the sunlight. Her blue eyes dominated her face, big and intelligent. She looked radiant and powerful, like a warrior goddess.

"Nice glamour," I told her.

"I want to set the right tone," she responded. "In case they want to start a battle."

Kara looked around the field. "I think we would win," she said.

Together, we faced the Gateway, an odd patch of earth with nothing special about it, other than with the right words and spells it would allow us to step between worlds. I rubbed my foot over a discarded white stone; last time, we'd placed a ring of the rocks around the Gateway, so we knew where it was. But over the last fifty years, the stones had moved, or fallen into the earth or become covered by vegetation.

I put out a hand, sensing the rocks and pushed them to the surface, cleaning dead grasses, dirt and, in one case, an anthill from them. I used my magic to roll them back into position.

"I'd forgotten we put those there," Rhena said. "And good idea. That way, we know where the Gateway is."

"Can't you feel it?" I asked. My skin hummed, an uncomfortable buzzing like being close to a beehive.

"Just a little," Kara said. "But only if I focus on it."

Behind us, the council members, Lord Saynor and his followers, took up their positions while Rhena folded her hands and nodded at the royal spell user. He said the incantation, picking up a potion and throwing it at the open space. The liquid caught, freezing in mid-air as the Gateway opened. Sparkles glittered in the sunlight and fog filled the valley. A wind blew our hair into our faces.

Finally, the Gateway opened. Like it always had, the Gateway showed a library, bookshelves and a large couch upholstered in blue still evident. But there wasn't anyone standing waiting for us. Had they not gotten our scroll?

After a moment of no movement through the Gateway, Rhena nodded at one of her guards. He walked toward the open Gateway inspecting the passageway. After a minute, he stuck the hilt of his spear through the opening.

Nothing happened. He withdrew it and looked at Rhena.

"Stick your head through," she said. "But be careful." The guard did so, his shoulders remaining in our world, his head in the other. It seemed as if we stared at the back of his head through a faint waterfall.

"We've never had to go through ourselves?' I asked.

Kara shook her head. "I don't think we have. I've never seen it written about what their world looked like."

"Why not?" Rhena asked. "Why have we never seen their world?"

"I don't think they ever invited us," I said. "Which is odd. Why did we never ask? Many of their people came through, and we never stepped foot in their world?"

The guard pulled his head back through and came to stand before us. He bowed. "It looks like a library," he said. "Lots of books on the shelves, a big desk with an odd gray box on it. There was no one there."

"Did you see our scroll?" Kara asked.

He nodded. "On the ground, the wax intact. I don't think anyone read it."

"Wonderful," Rhena said. "They didn't know we were coming and thus aren't prepared for trade."

"We need to find someone in their world," Kara said. "Find out if Lord Sebastian is still alive. If they're even interested in reopening the Gateway."

The council members shifted behind her, and no one spoke.

"Lady Larieda should go," Lord Saynor said. "With a glamour, she'd look human."

His eyes bored into mine; he hated me for voting to open the Gateway.

"I'll go," Kara said.

"Absolutely not," another council member replied. "Lady Kara is our primary potion maker and second in line to the throne."

"Lady Larieda is most expendable," Lord Saynor said. "Not an heir, and while valuable in the birthing room, her counsel is negligible."

Rhena's nostrils flared. This was a trap. Get us to fight amongst ourselves, and we wouldn't step through the Gateway.

"Lady Larieda is an important member of the council," Rhena began.

"And not expendable," Kara said, her cheeks heated.

We didn't have time for this.

Reaching within myself, I calmed my nerves and ran toward the Gateway. I heard Kara's yell, but it fell silent as I leapt through. I took a deep breath and stifled a cough, my throat closing in disgust. The air in the Contraries' world smelled of dust, metal, and burned chemicals. I made sure my hair covered my pointed ears and looked around.

The library was larger than it seemed from the part we'd seen through the Gateway. The entire room was double the size of my bedchambers in the castle, and completely lined with bookshelves, books and notebooks. There were even small, hip-high bookshelves set in the middle of the room, segmenting it.

Every shelf was full to capacity, books stacked on top of each other, and a giant wooden table sat in the middle of the room, a gray box in the middle, with various papers and writing implements surrounding it. A green armchair sat in the corner with a light-giving implement arced over it, a brightly colored quilt on the seat and trailing on the floor. A perfect reading spot. Bright sunlight filtered through the cracks behind a thick blue curtain, and dust motes sparkled, thick in the air.

"Hello?" I called out. "Anyone here?"

Silence.

Kara stepped through the Gateway with five guards

behind her. I could see Rhena through the Gateway, her hands on her hips, glaring at us.

"You're in trouble," Kara told me.

"This was more expedient than arguing."

We turned our back on the Gateway while one guard touched the desk, leaving trails from his fingers in the dust. Either no one had been in here in several weeks, or no one had cleaned recently or used the desk. A boom sounded in the distance, and the ground shook slightly, more dust flying into the air.

Odd. I couldn't imagine what would cause the deep, echoed sound. It reminded me a bit of the slamming of a door, but it felt far off. Perhaps this room was in a giant building.

I pulled a notebook off a shelf and opened it. I vaguely remembered being shown how to read the Contraries' alphabet before we'd closed the Gateway. It was roughly the same as ours; the same number of symbols in a similar style, though they didn't always apply in the same way. The Contraries also read the opposite way we did, left to right rather than right to left.

I recognized Father's name, though, and picked out Lord Saynor as well. In the top left corner were a few numbers separated by dots. Likely a date, though it made little sense to me. This must be a journal from before the Gateway was closed. There were dozens of them and upon inspection, appeared to outline each interaction with us. Someone had kept meticulous records; more meticulous than we had. I continued to pick up books at random, moving away from the notebooks and into the actual books. This writing was standardized and easier to read, every letter formed the same way.. I vaguely remembered a discussion of how the Contraries printed books for everyone to read rather than copying them as we did.

If we could keep the Gateway open this time, perhaps we

should look into understanding this process; we could expand our people's knowledge of magic and history tremendously.

Kara also picked up books at random, not able to read the alphabet, but looking for books with illustrations. I moved throughout the room, pulling back a curtain to look outside the window. I could see a tree and other buildings, gray and stone-like. The sky looked odd here, an orange that muted the light rather than the blue I was used to. Fog and smoke from chimneys floated between buildings.

The booming sound came again, closer. The windows shook and the metal cabinet jangled. Was this kind of sound normal? Perhaps it was thunder, but a different thunder than I'd ever heard.

"Look at this," one guard said, pointing at a framed picture on the wall. Kara and I came closer, studying the drawing. I recognized Father, a few council members, and even Rhena standing in her courtly dress, all of fifteen years old and about to inherit a kingdom at war with everyone else.

They'd devoted this room to us. So why hadn't there been a guard waiting for us to contact them? It had been a hundred years, but the amount of information in this room showed devotion. Why had no one been monitoring the Gateway?

Perhaps they'd given up, assuming after the death of Father we'd never want to come through again. And they'd be mostly right if we hadn't needed them so badly.

The door into the room opened, making me jump. One guard drew his sword with a quiet snick.

"Hello?" a soft voice called out.

The guards closed around Kara and me as a child stepped in. "Hello?" she said again. She held something wrapped in a blanket.

"Hello," I said back. She looked us up and down, eyeing the guards in their chest plates, helmets, and my blue and silver dress. She wore some sort of baggy-patterned pants that looked soft and a t-shirt with a picture of a cat on it.

Her eyes widened, and she stared over my shoulder. I turned around; you could see the field, the tents and even Rhena through the Gateway, like it was a glassed window. "Did you come through the mirror?" she asked.

"Mirror?" I turned around. The Gateway on this side had a large gold frame; perhaps when it was closed, it appeared as a reflective device.

"The Gateway?" Kara asked.

The child stepped further into the room, the wrapped blanket in her arms beginning to cry. It was a baby, I realized with a shock. What was this child doing with a baby?

"It's open," she whispered, jostling the baby like an auntie, trying to get it to relax. "Mr. Lucuis was right. They said he was just old when he told me the place behind the mirror was real. When people get old, their minds get tired and sometimes they lie, but don't know it. But he kept saying that if only the Gateway was open, we could get out. And we should pray for it."

The girl stepped closer to the Gateway, staring at Rhena through it.

"Is that a queen?"

"That's my sister," I said.

"Are you a princess?"

"No–" I shook my head, trying to focus.

"Do you know a Lord Sebatian?" Kara asked. "Can we talk to him?"

The baby wailed, and the little girl sat down in the armchair, pulling a bottle from her pocket and offering it to the baby. The baby sucked greedily, its hands clutching at the glass.

The girl shook her head, her eyes on the baby. "Slow down," she said. "That's all we have."

Where was the baby's mom? Surely it wasn't this little girl. Were there no other women who could nurse this baby?

"Lord Sebastian," I reminded her. "Do you know him?"

"He's dead," she said. "He had a heart attack a few days ago."

"I'm sorry," I said. "I hope he finds peace. Can we talk to Sebastian's children, your parents? Do they know about the gate—mirror?"

"Everyone knows," she said. "Some have been praying it would open, like Mr. Lucuis said to. He said it was the only way out of the city. But others are trying to find another way."

The boom sounded again, the entire building shaking. Kara let out a yelp. One window broke and books fell from their shelves. The girl encircled her body around the baby as the baby screamed.

"They're getting close," the little girl said. "We have to go."

"Go where?" I demanded.

"Through there," she said, pointing at the Gateway. "You came here to save us, right? Like Mr. Lucuis said."

"Save you?" Kara asked.

One guard took my arm as another boom shook the castle. Dust flew, and a bit of the ceiling came down. "We should go," he told me. "This is war."

"Let me get everyone," the girl said. "Here," she ran to me, passing me the baby. "Hold her and I'll go get everyone."

The baby stopped crying, staring up at me with giant green eyes. I stared back, my soul quieting, despite the shouts outside. "Lady Lareida," the guard said. "Put down the baby, we should go."

"No," I said, though another boom from far away made my heart pound. I cradled the baby against my chest, protecting it as the entire building shook around us.

Then the door to the library opened and people, so many Contraries, hurried in. It was mostly children, but a few women too, one waddling with pregnancy. They were skinny, bags under their eyes, with streaks of dirt and dust on their clothes.

They looked like the survivors of villages when my father had come through. I had no idea what was happening, but this place couldn't be safe for them.

"Hurry," I said, pointing at the Gateway. "Go through."

"Rhena won't be happy," Kara said.

"Would you let these people die? They need to get out of here."

"I know, I'm just saying she's going to be mad."

The little girl was the first one through. She ran to Rhena, pointing at us, no doubt trying to explain how she saw the Gateway as a mirror and that her people needed sanctuary. The guards helped those unable to do so step over the frame into Punthyn.

More people kept streaming into the room, children, teenagers, a few with babies. I tried to keep a rough count, but lost track around fifty.

The booms were getting more frequent, the dust making my eyes stream and my lungs fill. The last of the windows burst, glass shooting into the room. Contraries screamed, flinging their arms up to protect their faces. Outside, I heard more screams and an odd pulsing alarm. I should pass the baby off to another, but I didn't want to let her out of my sight.

The entire building shook, all the books on the shelves falling to the ground, one shelf tipping over completely.

"That's the entrance," a Contrary yelled as she ran in. "We have to go."

One guard grabbed my arm and pulled me through the Gateway, Kara a step behind. Behind us, the Gateway shook and closed. The royal spell users murmured and began waving their hands and chanting, trying to get the passageway to reopen.

Contraries were everywhere, sitting on the ground, pointing at the Gateway, at each other, or being led into tents. Some stared around them. Some cried. Some hugged each other.

"What did you do?" Rhena asked. "I had thought before you allowed the Contraries through we would've discussed it." The baby against my chest let out a sound, and I pulled the blanket away, inspecting the perfect little girl.

"I think there was war," I said. "In their world. Those people were hiding in that building. They were all about to die." I watched the castle spell users try to open the Gateway without success. "I think that library and the building it was in is destroyed," I said. "We saved all these Contraries."

The little girl came running up to me, and I passed her the baby. "I kept her safe," I told her, suddenly feeling a little lost without the child in my arms.

"Thank you," she said. "Her mama died a few days ago. She just has me."

"Where's your family?" Rhena asked.

"They all died," the little girl answered, cradling the baby. "My building got bombed, and Mr. Lucuis told me I could stay with them. He put me in charge of Isa. Told me to pray that the Gateway would open because it would be our only way to a new home. Is this our home?"

"Yes," Rhena said with a sharp nod. "This will be you and the others' new home. We'll ensure you and the rest of the Contraries are cared for. What is your name?"

"Rachel."

"Who is in charge of your people? I'd like to speak with them."

Rhena went off to find the leader, and I went to get Rachel something to eat, Kara trailing behind. I held Isa as Rachel stuffed bread, cheese, and strawberries into her mouth, barely swallowing. The little girl was ravenous, barely swallowing before she pushed more food into her mouth. These poor people had been so mistreated.

I was going to need to find Isa a wet nurse.

"Do most of the Contraries, the people you came with, not have families?" I asked Rachel.

She shook her head. "Most Mr. Lucuis found on the street and brought them to the house. He had plenty of food and shelter. And said the mirror would open and we would get out."

"So you're all orphans?"

Rachel nodded, swallowing and stuffing a strawberry into her mouth. Isa had fallen asleep in my arms and made a faint sigh of contentment. I couldn't get over the feeling of connection I had to this baby. I'd held hundreds of babies since Ivo's death and not a single one had spoken to my soul like this one had. It wasn't the same as Ivo–this little girl wasn't my baby's replacement. But it was like my soul knew this baby's soul. I wouldn't let anything happen to this baby or the other Contraries who had come through.

I looked at the baby in my arms. "Do you think you and Isa would like to live in a castle?" I asked. "My sisters and I could be your family, since you don't have any others." Where had that come from? It was like the words had come through unprompted.

"A real castle like out of a fairytale?"

"A real castle," I confirmed, unsure what a fairytale was.

"Isa too?"

"Of course."

"I'd love it!" Rachel said.

Isa woke up and stared up at me with her green eyes. I held her closer to my chest, rocking her as she stared up at me.

CHAPTER 4

THE WORLD MY CHILDREN LIVE IN

"HOLY MOTHER OF GOD," I yelled, dropping my hairbrush onto my dresser, where it ricocheted onto the laminate flooring of my bedroom with a bang. With a groan, I bent over to pick it up and smacked my head on an open drawer.

I'd been seeing Jacie within my bedroom mirror for months, but her sudden appearance always gave me heart palpitations. One of these days, she'd give me a heart attack. Probably sooner rather than later, judging from my cardiologist's report.

Rubbing the back of my head and straightening, I held up one finger to the other woman standing within the mirror and listened. Had my kids heard my yell or cared enough to check on me?

Judging from the silence in the kitchen where they were eating their breakfast, they didn't.

"I'm fine," I yelled. "In case either of you were worried."

"I wasn't," my thirteen-year-old son yelled back.

I rolled my eyes, my eyeballs practically hitting my brain. I wasn't going to survive his teenage years. Closing my bedroom door, I focused on the tall, dark-skinned woman, her curly hair twisted to the top of her head, wearing a green wool dress, and a dark apron. I didn't have to turn around to know she wasn't actually behind me; she was in the mirror, talking to me from a different world.

"Hey there!" I said. "Everything okay?" I leaned close to the mirror to brush on some blush. I tried not to be one of those moms who showed up for school drop-off looking like she'd just rolled out of bed.

"I sent you a note two days ago," Jacie said, crossing her arms against her ample chest. "Through the mirror. You didn't answer."

"Dang it," I said. My eight-year-old daughter had probably found the note and hidden it into her school backpack or under her bed. Guess it didn't matter; she wouldn't understand it. It was likely just another pretty envelope to collect, like the overdue electric bill I'd found in her sock drawer once. "I'm sorry," I said. "I didn't get it. What's going on?"

"You need to come back to your village, Celicia," the other woman said. "The witch's curse is getting worse. The wards are collapsing over all of our villages. You gotta come back and help us rebuild them."

"I was in Stirelli a week ago," I said. "I didn't feel like the curse was that bad. It felt like the wards were keeping it out." Mostly. I had seen the effects of the curse on my people; they'd been a bit more sedate, and many were slower in taking care of their farms, but it was springtime. No one wanted to work in the spring.

"About a third of my people are cursed now," Jacie said. "They just sit there staring off into the distance. Won't open their shops, won't farm, won't help their families. I mean, there are kids running around everywhere because their parents just don't care. The wards are the only thing that's protecting our villages. And they're getting weak. I have two people who stopped eating. Two! They're going to starve themselves."

My stomach lurched. I was responsible for my people. We

had a symbiotic relationship. Surely I would've felt it if my people stopped eating. "I didn't think things were that bad."

"Well, they are. Can you please come back today? I don't want more of my people to get cursed."

As the Maven of Stirelli, I handled my village and my people. When I was away from my village and even that world for too long, crops didn't grow, the chickens laid the eggs spoiled, and impossible things like witch curses happened. Additionally, too much time spent in this world, the world my children existed in, destroyed my health. I was on medications for cholesterol, low thyroid, and high blood pressure; medications I didn't need in Stirelli.

"I can't come today," I said. "The kids have dentist appointments this afternoon."

"A dentist appointment is more important than your people dying?" Jacie folded her arms across her chest.

"Has anyone died yet?"

"Not yet, but if they've stopped eating, they will."

"Do you know how hard it is to get an appointment anymore?" I said. "One of my kids has a toothache and even with that, it's taken three weeks to get to the appointment." I loved being a mother to my children and a Maven in Stirelli, but balancing the two worlds was hard.

"I'll come out tomorrow," I said. "One day won't make a difference. Two-minute warning," I yelled to my kids, my mom-voice echoing through the house.

"Please," Jacie said. "I'm so worried about my people. I can sense the wards breaking as the curse pounds into them."

"I know," I said. "I just… my kids."

"Please," Jacie said, putting her hands together in a praying motion. "There's always cancellations for dentists. You can get him in again. If your people die because—"

Oh god, I didn't want to be responsible for someone's death. My primary responsibility was to prevent deaths, not cause them.

"We'll meet you at the sacred pool," Jacie continued. "You need the power boost; you look like you're in your fifties. Besides, Ava visited the library at Mirfield. In theory, you can find anything there. Maybe she has news about how to get rid of the curse or who even cursed us. Some solution the scholars and librarians recommended."

"I know how to get rid of it," I said. "We curse the witch back."

"That's not our way."

"I know," I muttered. But I wished it was. Becoming a Maven had actually come with superpowers, though they didn't work in the world my kids lived in. In the other world, I could fly, I could heal, I could create power balls of energy. I knew where all my people were and could sense the general health of my village. But it was all instinctual, and becoming Maven hadn't come with an instruction manual. And Ava and Jacie said they didn't know how to curse anyone.

I put my hairbrush away, noting the gray hairs in the fibers.

"Please," Jacie whispered. I stared at the other woman in the mirror. In all the months I'd known her, I'd never seen her looking this defeated, her eyes sunken and her skin slightly gray. Her green dress sagged on her frame like she'd lost weight.

"Okay, okay, I'll cancel the dentist appointments. I'll be there after school drop-off."

"Thank you," Jacie said, fading away.

☺

"I'm just going to slow down, and you guys can hop out," I told my kids as I navigated through our suburban neighborhood in my SUV. Enormous houses on tiny lots, most with small soaking pools in the backyards, lined the streets. Teslas, BMWs, Audis, and Mercedes pulled out of garages as their owners started their morning commute. I braked hard to avoid a group of high school girls who stepped into the street without looking, too busy chattering and staring at their cell phones.

Now that I'd decided to go to Stirelli, my heart beat with, "hurry, hurry, hurry." Had the Healer been affected, or had he stopped checking on the ill and delivering babies? Were the farmers still harvesting crops? Had someone's livestock died from starvation? Were the children being taken care of? Now that I felt for it, I sensed my people's need; their desperation for a solution. They needed me.

But so did my kids.

Rather than joining the large drop-off line circling the block, I pulled in front of a house the same model as ours and pushed the button to open the doors. "Okay, get out," I said. "Oh wait, I'm sorry—that was rude. Please, get out."

"Here?" Ryder, my thirteen-year-old son, asked.

"Won't hurt you to walk."

"It might," he muttered. He'd forgotten to brush his midnight dark hair, and it stuck up at an odd angle against the back of his head. "A car could run off the road and hit us on the sidewalk. Someone could kick a ball in front of me, I trip in front of it and bam, hit my head. No more me."

I squelched the tiny wiggle of mommy fear. "I love your imagination," I said. "But nothing's going to happen. There's lots of kids walking from here and all of them will make it to school." I resisted the impulse to reach behind and smooth his mussed hair. "Go on," I said with a mock growl. "Out. Get. Out!"

Ryder climbed out, swinging his backpack onto his shoulders.

I turned to mock glare at my eight-year-old daughter, Mina. "Go to school," I said. "Your brother won't wait forever."

"I don't feel good," she muttered.

Seriously? She was doing this now?

"In what way?" I unbuckled my seat belt and twisted to feel her forehead. No fever.

"I don't know," she shrugged. "Just don't feel good."

Was she being bullied? Had she gotten into a fight with a friend? Did she have a test? Was she going to throw up? Did she have flesh-eating bacteria? The hardest part of parenting was trying to read your child's thoughts. If I let her go, would the school call asking for me to pick her up when I was in Stirelli with no cell reception?

"I gotta have more to go off of," I told her. "Otherwise, go to school."

"Let's go, dork," Ryder shouted, leaning into the car.

"Don't call your sister a dork," I said automatically. "Mina." I forced her to look at me. "I have a lot to do today. But if you're truly sick, you can stay home. But only if you're really sick."

She said nothing, just stared down at the ground.

"Mina, are you sick?"

"No," she muttered.

"Okay, then I need you to go to school."

"Okay. Fine." Mina said, enunciating each syllable as she undid her seat belt and climbed out of the car as slowly as possible. I put the car into park and joined them on the sidewalk. I felt her forehead again, and then gave her a hug, breathing in her personal scents of toothpaste, laundry soap, and that unidentifiable but unique earthy smell of my child. Snaking an arm out, I grabbed Ryder, holding him close.

Ryder withstood my arms around him for a whole five seconds before squirming away with a "jeez, Mom," but he couldn't duck his head fast enough to hide the smile. With her own inhale, Mina released me, nodded, then trudged after her brother. With their pale skin and dark hair, so similar to mine, everyone knew they were siblings.

Everyone knew they were my children, who looked nothing like their blue-eyed, blonde father.

I jumped back into the car, flipping a U-turn in the middle of the street and driving back to my house as fast as I dared. Unlocking the front door, I dumped my purse and grabbed the bag I kept hidden in the bottom of the walk-in pantry. I shimmied into my blue wool dress, the fabric scratchy against my modern, shaved, and lotioned skin. Whipping my hair into a loose braid, I finished it with a bit of blue ribbon, and laced up my leather boots, mud still on the soles. I had to get the stepladder to reach the small silver box from the top shelf over the fridge.

I'd found the portal to Stirelli one child-free night when Ted had his court-mandated night with the kids. The package of herbal pills, guaranteed to improve anxiety and depression I'd purchased from a random social media post had arrived and I needed them. So rather than sobbing myself to sleep, I'd popped a red pill in my mouth, chased it with a swallow of chardonnay and fell through the floor.

A few seconds later, groaning, many hands had helped me to my feet. They'd smiled, welcoming me. I'd looked around, staring in awe at the Renaissance-like kitchen with its giant brass pots bubbling over a fire, herbs drying on racks hanging from the ceiling, and pies oozing fruit stacked on giant tables they used as counters.

The villagers led me to two women, Jacie and Ava, Mavens of neighboring villages. They'd been waiting for me, they'd explained, waiting to put me in charge of Stirelli, my own village in this world where magic actually existed. They'd been waiting to give me super powers. These people, my villagers, wanted me around, wanted me to help them. And best of all, none of these people had known how a momentary indiscretion had destroyed my marriage. None of these people were picking sides, ignoring my text messages and uninviting me to events my husband also attended.

In that state of mind, I'd immediately agreed to become the Maven of Stirelli, never even questioning where I was or what was being asked. Jacie and Ava had passed me two pills, green and purple. I'd swallowed and collapsed onto the wooden floor as orgasmic power flooded my veins. I'd never felt pleasure like that. When my limbs functioned and I was done moaning, I had my powers and was officially a Maven.

Jacie and Ava showed me how to sense my people, how to cast power balls and how to fly. They'd taken me on a tour of my village, explaining how it was primarily a farming community, but there was time for some leisure activities too. I'd fallen in love with the village immediately. If someone had told me to create a village in my mind, it would've looked exactly like Stirelli, with cobblestone streets, brick one and two-story buildings, the names of businesses hanging from signs in front of doorways. There were bars, restaurants, clothing stores, hardware stores, a chocolate store, and even a bookstore.

That night, there was a massive celebration; I'd danced with everyone, eaten spice cakes flavored with a honey-like nectar, and drank bubbling concoctions. Everyone had been so happy to meet me, to greet me, to ask my opinion on everything. It had been the best night of my life, better than my wedding, than my children's birth, than the time I'd gotten my master's degree.

The next morning, Jacie and Ava had handed me a silver box full of blue pills I could use to go back home, to go back to my children. And with the help of those blue pills and the red "herbal" ones from that social media ad, I'd spent the last six months jumping between worlds, trying to figure out how to balance my children's needs with Stirelli's. It helped that Ted, my ex-husband, couldn't stand to be in the same room with me, so when the kids were with him, I was free to spend the time how I wanted.

And I wanted to spend my time in Stirelli.

I took one last look at my phone; no message from Mina's school nurse demanding pickup. But her class would barely be starting. There hadn't been enough time for the teacher to worry, unless Mina had thrown up, or fainted, or something. Glancing at my kitchen table, I confirmed the placement of a letter, telling my kids I loved them, my wallet, phone, and a list of the passwords to various websites, including banking. I'd also left a letter to Ted, giving him full custody and willing all my assets to him until the children were eighteen. Ted hated me, but he'd do what was best for the kids.

I pulled a red pill out of the box. There were only two left. I needed to ask Jacie and Ava where to get more since it didn't seem like they were available online anymore. Dry-swallowing the pill, I closed my eyes and focused on the kitchen in the manor house I owned, thinking about the giant worktable and the herbs drying on the drying rack. The world spun around me, nausea filling my throat, and I fell through the floor.

I opened my eyes. Power filled me in an almost orgasmic burst as magic flooded through my veins. I tapped my fingers together, tiny arcs of blue lightning shooting out of them.

It was mid-afternoon, the sunlight glinting off copper pots stacked on the work table and the smell of a stew scenting the air. Fresh bread sat on racks close to the window, ready for the evening meal.

"You're late, Maven Celicia." Bethany, the woman who ran the manor house, said. "Maven Jacie said you'd be here an hour ago."

"I know, I know," I said. "I just had to do school drop off."

Bethany's face fell, and she inclined her head. I could see her scalp through her thinning blonde hair. Guilt bubbled up, and I winced. I hadn't meant to snap, but somehow it had come out that way. Time to be more careful. It wasn't her fault I was having a bad day. Bethany ran the manor house well, keeping it tidy, and dealing with a Maven who couldn't spend all of her time in Stirelli.

"I'm sorry," I said. "But I'm here now, and I'm focusing on being the Maven. I'm meeting Jacie and Ava at the sacred pools. We're going to rebuild the wards, and I have to hurry." I didn't add that the reason I had to hurry was so I could do school pick-up.

"The bookseller didn't open her doors," Bethany said. "Or the apothecary."

"I'm sorry," I said. "If I have time today, I'll check on them once I'm back from the sacred pools."

The woman folded her arms against her chest, puffing it out and glaring into my eyes.

"That's not good enough," she said.

"It's going to have to be," I said. "Let me get the wards back up, and I'll figure it out from there."

She deflated, a tear running down her cheek. "You need to be here," she said. "Your people need you."

"I know," I said. It was an old argument. She felt I needed to spend more time in Stirelli, and she didn't hear me when I tried to explain how my kids needed me, too.

"I know it's hard," I said. "But Jacie, Ava, and I are trying to fix the curse. Maven Ava just got back from Mirfield. Maybe she has news."

"Mrs. Loonts died," Bethany said.

"May her memory live on," I said, intoning the words they'd taught me for this world. "What happened?" I remembered the plump and pleasant woman who painted the lovely murals on the walls of so many of the buildings. She always had paint in her hair and sometimes would work herself to exhaustion.

"She stopped caring," Bethany said. "Stopped painting. She stopped eating. Then she wouldn't get out of bed."

The worst had happened. Someone had actually died from the curse. My hands fisted into balls, and I accidentally released an arc of blue magic, leaving a scorch mark on the wall.

"Are there any more?"

Bethany nodded. "Many won't eat."

"Okay," I said. "Let's assemble a group to go house to house, identify who is affected. Of those affected, let's work with their families to get them to eat. Maybe make their favorite food, spoon soup in their mouth." It worked with my kids, though I suspected it may not work with adults.

Bethany's face twitched, but she just nodded. "I'll begin immediately."

"Thank you," I said. "I will rebuild the walls and return tomorrow to speak to my people." Saying my goodbyes, I stepped outside, my boots sinking into the soft soil. The manor house, my house as the Maven of Stirelli, sat on a hill overlooking a valley full of my people's homes. I stared into the valley, a sense of calmness and serenity filling me. I breathed in deep the cinnamon and sage scented air. In this world, the sky was a purplish-blue, with sharp-peaked gray mountains stretching higher than I could see, their tops obscured in apricot clouds. Blue-grass, sharp enough to cut bare feet, filled the valley between the farms, grazed on by deer-like animals with thick tongues, orange and red coats and dozens of thin antlers, curling around their heads like some sort of mane. Afternoon sunlight filled the valley, bringing shades of colors we didn't have at home into sharp relief. Not for the first time, I wished I could bring a camera to take a picture. But anything that needed electricity, even if it was battery-powered, failed as soon as I arrived here.

I closed my eyes, focusing on the power beating through my heart and rolling through my veins and arteries. If I cut myself in this world, you could actually see the power, glittering quartz-like bits flowing through my blood. I took a deep breath, centering myself, locking away my emotions. Darkness fluttered against my closed lids, like the sun had gone behind a cloud. The bird song from the odd dragonfly-like hummingbirds stopped, and the feel of the cool breeze on my skin faded. Finally, the cinnamon and sage scent disappeared.

I opened my eyes.

Black ichor coated the valley, floating on the wind like spiderwebs, covering everything in black tar. A door closed behind me, and I watched Bethany crossing the field into the stables. The bright greens, yellows, and purples of her life force puddled at her feet, sinking into the earth. She too was cursed. We needed to stop this curse, or I'd lose everyone in Stirelli.

Thirty minutes later, I stepped into the darkened cave with the sacred pool. Focusing my magic, I lit up the blue crystals in the walls; the color joining Jacie's green and Ava's yellow. The light from the crystals created an odd patchwork of colored light against the walls, the pool, and the rocks. Water, the source of the pool, dripped from a ceiling shrouded in darkness. We didn't know how deep the pool was, but no creature stirred the depth of the water.

The normally clear water was brown tinged with the blood from Ava and Jacie's sacrifices. Nodding at them, I picked up a blue crystal, lifted my skirt and made a slight cut against the inside of my thigh where no one would see it. I coated the crystal with blood and dropped it into the pool, watching the blood float away.

Magic punched through us, and we gasped in unison as the power from the pool and our sacrifices filled and fueled our bodies. Those few seconds of euphoria were better than any drug, any sex, and yet were only echos of the night when I'd promised to be a Maven. Jacie and Ava joined hands with me, power crackling and rippling out from us, blue for me, green for Jacie, and yellow for Ava. Power arcs hit the cave walls, ricocheting and making the earth rumble. Sparkling dust from the walls filled the air, and we breathed deep, the cinnamon smell increasing our powers until we couldn't take in anymore.

"Let's begin," Ava said as we focused on the wards. Hours passed as together, we rebuilt the wards, a complex web of our powers, and pushed it out, covering and protecting our villages.

Finally depleted, we collapsed to the ground, panting with effort and with the loss of our magic. After a few minutes, I rolled into a sitting position. "I know I say this every time, but we really need to bring pillows with us."

Jacie sat up on an elbow, her curly hair mussed around her face, and smiled ruefully. "You keep forgetting."

Ava sat up gracefully, pulling her legs around her into a lotus position, her hands open on her knees. Ava was about twenty years older than Jacie and me, though she didn't look like it. She was an odd duck, but a useful one, and I needed her knowledge and experience. Without speaking or even greeting me, she closed her eyes, breathing deeply. Taking the hint, we did the same. I stretched out with my powers, feeling for the inter-webbing of the wards over our villages. I sensed the blues, greens, and yellows of our colors stretching out, interlacing, from the pool to envelope our villages. The ichor faded away, held at bay for the moment.

I opened my eyes, air-high-fiving the other two women. Jacie air high-fived me back and Ava ignored me, her amber eyes glowing in the light from the pool.

"As we know, we've been cursed," Ava said, with no preamble. "But in Mirfield, I found out who cursed us." She paused, picking up a yellow crystal to caress between her fingers.

I spun my hand in a flippy motion, telling her to speed it up. Ava could be overly dramatic.

"It's the king's witch," she intoned.

"Why?" I asked. "That makes no sense."

Ava shrugged and tossed her crystal into the water. I watched it sink past where I could see it. "The king wants our sacred pool."

Jacie gasped. "Can he use it? I mean, I guess maybe his witch can."

"Wait," I said. "Why would they curse us with such a slow curse? Why not curse us with a sickness that kills everyone in two hours? Or just attack? He has an army."

"It's likely easier," Ava said. "Perhaps they're just waiting for all of us to die. Then they don't have to mount an attack and risk their people. And I think the curse has been with us for a while, building up power. Now that we've realized it's here, it's almost too powerful to stop."

"This is ridiculous," I said. "Why would a king destroy his own people?"

"It's not like where you come from," Jacie said. "The king here is horrible. He enjoys hurting us."

"So what do we do? You found the answer, right?" I glanced at my analog watch, the special one I'd bought so I wouldn't be late for Mina and Ryder. Only one hour before school pickup. I hated being pulled in so many directions. But at least the wards were back up, my people safe.

One crisis at a time.

Ava shook her head. "Once the librarians found out the king cursed us, they locked me out of the library."

Jacie let out a puff of air. "God, what are we going to do?"

"I've been reflecting on it and perhaps we should give the pool to the king and his witch," Ava said. "The wards won't last forever, and that would save our people. We could start our villages again elsewhere."

"Can we do that?" I asked. "I think we need the sacred pool to survive, right?"

Ava shrugged. "We may not have our powers anymore, but our people would be safe."

"I don't believe that," Jacie said. "Without our powers, what's stopping the king from destroying our villages just for fun? Maybe we find some perfect farm land and he decides he wants that too, so he sends a new curse."

I looked at my watch again. I had to get back. "Look, we bought some time," I said. "I love my village, and it would break my heart to leave it. But I'll come tomorrow, and we'll do some planning. Some of my people are cursed, and I need to speak to them anyways. Get them to eat."

"How many pills do you have left?" Ava asked. "You have to be nearly out."

I smacked my forehead. "I keep forgetting to ask. Can I have some more, please?"

"You can't," Ava said. "Once they're gone, they're gone."

Wait, what? My heart dropped into my stomach.

"How many more do you have?" Jacie asked.

"One red, two blue. What happens to Stirelli if I don't come back?"

"Another Maven appears," Ava said. "But it's hard on your people and affects your village. You may not realize it, but your farmland isn't as good as ours. You don't have as many people and your buildings aren't as nice, because Stirelli's been through three Mavens in five years."

"What do you mean, my village's been through three Mavens in five years?" I asked.

"It's been hard," Jacie said. "I mean, not everyone wants to give up their life to stay here."

"Yeah, I get that," I said. "So… once I'm out of pills, I can't come back?" Jacie and Ava nodded. The idea of never seeing the apricot clouds, of never seeing my people, of never seeing the sun set over my forest broke my heart. "God, this sucks," I said. "And I have to leave it when everyone is cursed. Why didn't you guys tell me?"

Ava and Jacie exchanged a look. "It's complex," Ava said. "But we've found this is the best way. This way you've made an educated choice. You've spent time in Stirelli, you know the people, and you know how much they depend on you."

"I do, but my children come first. So now you're forcing me to choose between them and that's not ok."

Jacie nodded. "It's been a terrible choice for us too, but…" She smoothed back loose strands of her hair. "But we had to try something different.'

"And not telling me was something different."

"It was my call," Ava said. "I chose not to tell you."

"Are you sure I can't get more pills?" I asked. "Maybe I can help transition a new Maven."

"We're positive," Ava said. "So you're choosing the other world."

"Of course," I said. "It's going to destroy me, but I can't leave my kids. And I can't bring them here?"

Ava shook her head. "They can't cross without a pill. You holding their hands while you take yours won't do any good. You'd leave them behind."

"I tried it," Jacie said softly. "Didn't work."

"Okay then," I said with a sharp nod. "You both suck, but I'll come back tomorrow and say my goodbyes." God, this was going to feel like ripping out my soul; I just knew it.

Jacie licked her lips. "Your kids will grow up without a mother, whether you stay or go."

"Excuse me?"

"If you stay in their world, you'll die soon." Ava said. "Do you have cancer yet?"

"God no!" I felt nauseous, anxiety bubbling up to fill my throat.

"You will," Ava continued. "If you stay here, you can say goodbye to your children, and live many years longer than you would back there."

"As the Maven," Jacie said, fondling a green crystal. "The

village becomes your family. And you get all the power. And your abilities just keep growing and growing."

I didn't want power, I wanted to watch my kids grow up. I loved Stirelli, but my kids came first. I wanted to watch Ryder and Mina graduate from high school and college, fall in love, maybe have kids. Was I going to miss that, no matter which world I chose? Tears filled my eyes, and I accidentally shot a stream of blue energy into the cave wall. "Why didn't you tell me? I wouldn't have agreed to stay here!"

"No, you wouldn't have," Ava said, her amber eyes boring into mine. "None of us would have. But you wouldn't have come here if you weren't ready for a change. If you didn't want a different life. The pills only go to those who want a change. Those who want to be a Maven."

"I'd just gotten divorced because I fucked another guy in his backseat at the library after I dropped the kids off. Of course, I wanted a change. But that doesn't mean I don't want to live in the same world as my kids." I was weeping now, snot running from my nose. I ran a shaking fist underneath it.

"It's easier to find out this way," Jacie said. "Like ripping off a bandaid."

"And it's still a choice," Ava said. "You can stay in the world with your kids for as long as you survive."

"How long do I have in that world?"

Ava shook her head. "Until your body gives out. Couple months probably. It won't be a nice way to die. But you would still have your kids."

"How am I supposed to decide this?" I sobbed. "I either give up my kids or I die."

Jacie touched my arm. "Go home. You have a bit of time. I'll send you notes through the mirror telling you what's going on with your people until you decide. Stirelli will be safe for the time being. The wards will hold, and we'll help take care of your people."

"Our villages come first," Ava said with a sharp look at

Jacie. "Our villages are cursed too." Her face softened as I let out a sob. "But we'll try," she said.

"You're both horrible people," I said. "You tricked me."

"Yes," Ava said, her directness making me hate her even more. "But it's the only way to get Mavens. We made the same choice. We have the same regrets. I have grandchildren back in your world I've never met. I miss my husband, my friends and my children every day. But our villages and hundreds of people are alive because I chose my village."

"And your village needed a Maven," Jacie said. "It was floundering without one. And we could sense something on the horizon, a sickness maybe, or a drought–"

"Or a curse," Ava said.

"Or a curse," Jacie echoed. "We knew your village wouldn't survive without a Maven to build it up before it hit. I don't know. We probably did this the wrong way."

"Probably?" I asked. "Now I have to leave my village without a Maven and during the middle of a curse. And you both expect me to choose my village over my children."

"We expect you to choose living over death," Ava said.

I glanced at my watch. I had to go. Without saying anything, I ran out of the cave, back to my blue pills, back to my children.

☙

"I can't believe you didn't come and get me." Mina was in sobby tears in the backseat of the SUV. I'd missed multiple calls from the school nurse asking me to come and get my daughter after she'd thrown up twice. Then missed multiple calls from Ted, telling me the school had contacted him and reminding me he was on a business trip, two time zones away and couldn't get Mina. Then I missed a phone call from my ex-mother-in-law, telling me the school had called her to pick up Mina and she could not do so. Then I had a last phone call from Ted, chastising me yet again for making my momentary indiscretion a year ago more important than our children. And that if I hadn't cheated on him, and if he hadn't needed to support two households, he wouldn't be two time zones away, and I could keep doing whatever I thought was more important than our children.

I truly was a terrible parent. I'd chosen to be a Maven, the fun and adventure of a totally different world over them. And I hadn't known the price. I'd should've asked. I should've known it was too good to be true.

"I'm sorry," I said for the fifteenth time. "I forgot to plug in my phone, was running around with errands and hadn't even realized it had died."

It was a sucky lie, and judging from the narrow-eyed glare from Ryder, he knew it. I adjusted my sunglasses. A terrible headache, complete with stabby pains from the sunlight, destroyed my focus. I could barely drive. Riffling in my purse, I dry swallowed another two ibuprofen, though I'd already taken four. Maybe my liver would be the first to go.

"Let's get you a snack and maybe into the bathtub with a magic fizzer," I told Mina. "Then we see how you feel about theater rehearsal." I needed to enjoy every minute, needed to give them a perfect life for as long as I could.

Back in the house, I got Mina some watered-down chicken noodle soup and ran a warm bath in my tub with her favorite grape-scented bath bomb. She still didn't have a fever and said her stomach was better after eating. Maybe I'd keep her home tomorrow rather than going by to Stirelli. Maybe I'd keep them both home. Maybe I'd give them a break from school for a while; do all the things we never had time to do.

But they needed school too, needed the structure, needed to learn math and sciences or they'd never succeed in life. Holy God, this was a terrible choice.

I mediated Ryder's homework and asked a neighbor to take him to and from soccer so I could stay with Mina. By the time he was home, though, she was better, and I took them both to theater rehearsal. I spent the lesson working with the other moms on costumes, trying to make the most of my time, create some memories for my kids, though my headache was so bad my hands shook, and I was in a terrible mood. I kept trying not to scream at these women, obsessing over whether a sequined belt was appropriate for a seven-year-old, that none of this mattered. My kids wouldn't have a mom much longer and who cared about a stupid belt!

After rehearsal, we pulled into the driveway to a darkened house. God-damn-it, I'd forgotten to leave any lights on. I was usually better than this, but with the migraine pounding against my head, I was happy I remembered how to drive. The kids leapt from the car, running up the driveway, unlocking the front door, and disappearing inside. I stayed in the car, trying to get the energy to step out. I should cook them something, something that would help Mina's stomach. Maybe their favorite meal. Pasta? Spaghetti? But it was after seven, and I wasn't sure I had it in me.

They loved pizza, though it probably wasn't the best for Mina's stomach. Waffling, I placed an order on an app, Ryder's garlic special and Mina's favorite with pepperoni and mushrooms. If she didn't want it, she could eat it tomorrow for dinner, and it wasn't fair to punish Ryder.

I grabbed their equipment bags and walked through the open door, the blazing lights from the entryway and living room lighting up the dark porch.

I flicked off the lights as I passed them. "Pizza is on its way and should be here in thirty minutes. Can one of you set the table?" I called. "I don't care who."

Expecting groans and "not-its!" The silence surprised me.

"Dudes?" I called. "Seriously, could use help with the table. I've got a killer headache."

Lugging the equipment bags into the living area, I tripped over Ryder's hockey stick, landing with a sprawl. Son-of-a-bitch, that hurt. I straightened up, the ache in my hip and knee adding to the wailing in my head. Ryder hadn't played hockey in over a year. Why had he gotten out his hockey stick? And then just left it in the middle of the living room?

"Mina! Ryder!" I added the mom-snap at the end. "Not the time to play hide and seek!"

Limping, I turned a corner into the family room and stopped. The place was a mess, cushions ripped from the couches and a forgotten water glass shattered.

"What the hell?" I yelled. An arm raked around my waist, yanking me against a hard chest. With a yell of rage, I stomped on the person's foot and strained forward.

The arms released with a groan, and I spun around. A man in a doublet, a leather vest, and high boots pulled out his sword with a swish of metal. Where had he come from? He had to have come from Stirelli. No one I knew in this world would carry a sword. But I also knew he wasn't one of my people. Was he Jacie's or Ava's? Had they sent him? Why had he grabbed me?

"Where are my children?" I clicked my fingers together, more habit than anything, and yelped when a tiny burst of blue power lit the room. There was magic! It was a tiny seed, but still there. I reached deeper, feeling my knees buckle as I tried to pull forth more power.

He nodded toward the small bathroom, the door closed, a chunk of wood from the kitchen table wedged in the crack between the floor and the door.

"Ryder, Mina?" I called. "Knock if you're okay." A faint knock sounded, and I sighed in relief. "Stay there guys, I've got this."

I got the tiny spark of power to build, the blue light glinting off his sword. "How did you get here?" I demanded.

He spoke, but it was gibberish, a language I'd never heard.

I worked to build the energy into a ball I could throw and

knock him out, ask questions later, but my vision doubled, and I had to fight the urge to sway. My ball fizzed out. Maybe I should make a dive for the hockey stick, hit him over the head and knock him out.

Ok, good plan.

"Who are you?" I demanded again, trying to distract him.

He opened his mouth to speak, but I didn't wait, lunging for the hockey stick. He caught me around my middle, lifting me off my feet. I yelled, kicked, and punched.

I would not let him win!

Blue and red lights suddenly lit up the street, streaming in through the windows. The front door vibrated with knocks.

"This is the police," someone shouted on the other side.

I screamed, like a teenager in a horror movie, and the cops burst through the door.

I hugged Ryder and Mina to me. Mina trembled like a leaf, but Ryder was stoic, his back straight and his shoulders hard with anger. I was more worried about him than Mina.

"I just came into the house," I told the cop taking my statement. "I was ordering a pizza on my phone, you know, using one of those apps, and just let the kids run into the house. When I came in, I saw him."

"Did he say anything?" the cop asked. She stared at me, eye to eye, looking for any hint of a lie, of my story changing.

"I didn't understand him," I said. "I asked where my kids were, and…" I passed a shaking hand through my hair. "Did he say anything? Why my house? I've never seen him before. I don't know why he attacked us."

"Just gibberish," the cop said. "And then you tried to pick up the hockey stick?" she prompted.

"Yeah. I don't—"

"I grabbed it," Ryder interrupted, telling his side. "When

we came in, he snatched Mina and put her in the bathroom. But I got away and grabbed my hockey stick from the closet. He took it away and threw me into the bathroom with her."

"We heard mom," Mina whispered. "She told us to stay there."

"That's a good mom," the cop said. "She did exactly right. You all did." Ryder sat up straighter. I was so proud of him. "And you're all sure you've never seen him before?"

We shook our heads.

"So who called the police?" the cop continued.

"I did," Ryder said. "He didn't take our phones."

The cop kept asking questions over and over, trying to get details we might have forgotten, while I held Mina against me.

Yes, the front door was locked when we'd come in.

No, I did not know how this person had gotten in, especially after the cops confirmed everything was locked up.

No, it didn't seem like anything was missing.

No, I didn't know who the man was or what he wanted.

Finally, she ran out of questions and closed her notebook. "We'll increase the patrols over the next few weeks, just in case, but we'll book the guy for breaking and entering. We can't understand him, but based on his sword, I bet he was doing a reenactment somewhere and took some drug. Thinks he's from another place. These geeks… they take this fan stuff way too seriously."

I gave her a weak smile and a nod.

"I'd make sure everything you lock everything up though," she told me as the rest of the cops finished whatever it was they were doing and left.

"I will," I said, finally pulling myself away from Mina and following the cops out to the front porch.

Neighbors had gathered, drawn by the light and perp walk of someone from my house. I knew if I jumped on the neighborhood social media, there would be dozens, if not hundreds of comments, asking for information, while others tried to guess what had happened. Domestic disturbance was probably the winner.

I gave a quick wave to them and shut the door. Telling Mina and Ryder to pack a bag, I started calling the parents I knew, finding friends Mina and Ryder could spend the night with.

I had one red pill left, and one blue one to come back again. I was going to Stirelli, to warn Jacie and Ava someone had made it through to our world, say my goodbyes, and come back. I'd made my choice. My kids were more important than Stirelli. I wasn't going to let anyone threaten them again. I wasn't going to miss dentist appointments or phone calls from the school again. I was going to repair my relationship with Ted so we could be cordial. I was going to be the best mother I could for as long as I could.

☙

I arrived to a full battle in my manor kitchen. The giant worktable had an ax through it, and a small fire burned in one corner, set off by magic spells. The air smelled of magic, metal, and smoke. I breathed in a lung-full and started coughing. Bethany came at me with a frying pan, and I threw up an arm just before she stopped.

"Maven Celicia," she wailed. "Make them stop!"

I pulled Bethany out of the way of a man with a sword. Bethany hit him in the arm and then the head with the frying pan. Down he went. A child wielding a butcher knife gave a guttural cry and took a wild swing at another man with a sword. The man stepped out of the way, swinging down at the child.

Power and ecstasy flooded my heart and blood, and I wrenched my hands apart, creating the energy ball I hadn't been able to make in my children's world. I launched it at the man the child fought and watched him collapse to the ground.

"Get out of here!" I said to the child. "Head for the forest!"

I launched three more energy balls. The men that didn't belong in my house fell to the ground.

More men wearing doublets and carrying swords ran in through the splintered doorway. Judging from the wooden crates and barrels littering the floor, they'd tried to shore up the room; protect those inside. With one thought, I shoved the attackers out and set up a magical barrier. It wouldn't hold for long, but it would work for now.

"Mavens Ava and Jacie are outside," Bethany said. "They came when we called. Band together and fight off this threat!"

Great idea.

"Thank you. All of you," I said to those in the room. "Head for the forest. This is not worth losing your lives over."

Outside of the kitchen were more fights, more men with swords, more people fighting with pieces of furniture. I launched blue power balls, downing the attackers and telling my people to get out, to head for the forest. Power sung in my veins, and with a sick lurch, I realized I enjoyed hurting the attackers. I enjoyed the rush of power, enjoyed protecting my people.

Perhaps this goodbye was meant to be. Maybe this was the best way to go, protecting those I was responsible for. Within a few more minutes, the attackers had all run off or were dead or injured.

"Let's lock up anyone still alive," I told Bethany. "We have a jail for a reason."

Spotting Ava and Jacie where they helped an elderly woman onto a rock, I went over to them. "Thank you both for coming to help Stirelli. What happened?"

Ava shook her head, moving us away from the villagers. "I don't know. One of your people sent up the green signal fire that your town was being attacked. I don't even know where the attackers came from. I think they're the King's men, they're wearing the livery–"

"I thought the king would wait until we're weak from the curse," I said.

She shook her head. "Maybe the king got bored. Or tired of waiting. Or thought you were weak enough."

"My god," I said. "But here's the worst part; I think one of the king's men made it through to my world," I said. "He attacked me and my kids in the house. He wore the same stuff as these guys."

"How?" Ava asked.

"And are they okay?" Jacie asked.

"They're fine," I said. "Scared, but–" I shook my head. "I don't know how that guy made it through."

Ava tugged on her lip. "Where do you keep your blue pills?"

"In the manor kitchen, in the pantry. I have one left. Which means this is goodbye. But I'll stay until we clean things up. The kids are fine for the moment."

Jacie and Ava exchanged a look. "Let's go find your pills," Jacie said, her voice shaking a bit.

The kitchen in the manor house was a disaster. Bits of broken furniture and smashed food were everywhere. Bethany worked with some villagers to tie up the attackers and ordered the men in the king's livery carried out of the room. Greeting her, we hurried into the pantry. Luckily, that space was still intact; the attackers hadn't made it inside. I reached up to the top shelf between bags of flour and sugar and jars of pickled beets to the small box that held my pills.

It wasn't there.

I searched on the other shelves.

Nothing.

"Help me," I asked the other Mavens. "It's a silver box. It must have gotten moved."

Ava began to search, pulling items off shelves, but Jacie stared at Bethany. Bethany stared at the floor.

"Bethany? Jacie?" I asked. "What's going on?"

"Did you give another Celicia's pills?" Jacie asked.

Bethany didn't answer.

"Did you?" Jacie snapped.

Bethany raised her chin and nodded once. "I knew if I sent another into your world, you would come."

My stomach seized. "He attacked me! My children!" I yelled.

Bethany stared at me. "I would not lose another Maven. You're too important to Stirelli. We need you."

"My kids need me," I whispered. "I need more pills."

"There aren't anymore," Bethany said. "This is your home."

Nausea rose. "My kids need a mom. You trapped me here. It was supposed to be my choice!"

"Oh my god, Celica," Jacie said, her hand going to her mouth. "I'm sorry."

"I need more pills," I said. "Please." I grabbed onto Ava's hands. "Please," I said. "I didn't get to say goodbye. They're going to think I just left them, that I didn't love them enough to stay."

Ava shook her head, a tear reflecting in her amber eyes. "I don't know of any way to make that happen. I'm so sorry. The choice should've been yours."

"You can send a note at least," Jacie said. "Better than nothing."

I spun around to Bethany, blue electricity arcing out of my body. "Get out," I screamed. "I don't want to see you ever again." My energy shot a hole into a wall, and someone outside screamed. "Get out!" I raged. "I forbid you to come to Stirelli ever again." Power built in my chest, and I pushed it through my veins, words I didn't know falling from my lips.

"From this moment, you are an exile. I will no longer see you, and no one in Stirelli will either."

I spun to Ava and Jacie, whose faces had gone ashen. "Do you know what you just did?" Ava hissed.

"Solved a problem."

"No one will see her. We won't see her. Her family will forget her. She can't get food, help–" Jacie said.

I couldn't deal with that now. I had to get back to my children. "How do I get to Mirfield?" I demanded. "Someone there has to know how to get back to my world and back to my children."

CHAPTER 5
A WAY OUT

"ALL I KNOW IS we're supposed to get out of the house." I brandished my phone at the other two adults. I had no bars, but we'd all woken up to the same text message: *The challenge is to find a way out!*

"It's like getting out of the Haunted Mansion at Disneyland," Yvonne said.

I raised an eyebrow.

"You know, like when you're in the elevator on that ride? The ghost host says it, right before the ceiling disappears and the lights go out." She pushed her glasses up her nose and hunched her shoulders. "It's my favorite ride," she muttered.

"Mine too," I said. And she was right; it was a direct quote from the amusement park.

I looked over at the other person in the room. Michael was in his forties wearing a sports blazer that practically screamed second date. "I haven't been in years," he said. "No idea about the scripting for some kid's ride."

"Well, that's something we don't have in common," Yvonne said. "Why are we here? Who brought us here?"

It was the fifth time she'd asked, and we still had no answers. I licked my parched lips and coughed a bit. My mouth felt like someone had stuffed it with cotton after they'd poured sand down my throat.

The three of us, Michael and Yvonne and I, had woken up in a decrepit nursery, in a house none of us claimed to have ever seen, each of us in one of the tiny single beds with rotting blankets pulled up to our chins. There'd been a mobile over mine, with horses jumping over hedges. Most were missing their heads, the bits having rotted off.

I fought the urge to shiver.

We'd done the where-are-we, who-are-you nonsense already. I was a broke college student slinging coffees at four a.m., named Jane. Yvonne was an elementary school librarian, and Michael "worked in healthcare" but wouldn't say what he did. I was betting he was a pharmaceutical sales guy that peddled expensive drugs patients couldn't pay for, but that docs prescribed to get free vacations.

None of us remembered how we got here, but we'd all been coming home, me from a night out with a friend, Michael from a date, and Yvonne from a book club.

I'd barely resisted rolling my eyes when she'd said that; she was such a walking cliche in her glasses, one inch heels, and blouse actually tied at the throat with a bow.

"We don't know why we're here," I told Yvonne again, running my hands through my hair and resisting the urge to yank on it. My skin hummed with an almost painful tingle, like a limb going to sleep. There was a ghost nearby. We needed to get the fuck out of this house.

"Let's go explore," I said. We didn't even know whether it was day or night; the windows in this room were boarded up, with no light getting through. "Maybe the downstairs windows aren't boarded up or there's a back door or something."

"Yeah, I told you," Michael said. "When I woke up, the front door was the first place I tried. It's locked, with giant sheets of plywood nailed against the opening, like there's a hurricane or something. I threw a chair against it, and it didn't even wiggle. I'm not even sure it's a real front door."

Well, that made no sense. I was trapped in this house with two morons. Perfect.

"Okay," I said. "No front door. We find another way out. We got in here somehow. It's not like we magically appeared. Someone locked us in and then left." At least I hoped they'd left. Maybe they were watching us from some weird cameras or holes in the walls.

I leaned close to a creepy horse painting, but no one was peeking out from the horse's eyes. Maybe the room was simply bugged. I should look for a smoke detector or a little flashing light.

"We need to figure out the why," Yvonne said, and I refocused on her. "Why would someone trap us together here? Something has to link us together."

A memory nibbled on the edge of my mind; a light coming at me in the darkness. A loud sound and fear, bubbling up, my heart jumping with it. I closed my eyes, chasing the memory. What was it? Something I remembered from a nightmare? Something from the person who drugged us and trapped us here?

The bit of memory floated away. Gone. It was probably some side effect from the drugs they'd given us.

"Yvonne, let's just focus on getting out," I said, releasing the hold on the memories. "Let's go room by room. Michael, what did you see when you tried the front door? Like how many rooms? Any windows?"

He shook his head. "It was really dark; just some faint ceiling lights on. But the hallway outside this room ends in a staircase, one of those curving ones you see in old houses. All the windows are boarded up, like in here." He ran a shaking hand through his mussed hair. "When I went down, the front door was right there. The chair I threw was this old thing with the carvings on the back. Super heavy. I don't know, felt like we were in a fancy house. The furniture looked old, but I didn't really look. I just tried to find the front door."

"Okay, let's just do this assembly-line style," I said. The humming in my skin was getting worse; my brain felt like it was vibrating within my skull. "Check every room, look for doorways and windows, then move on to the next one. Maybe this is just some fucked-up escape room game and we'll find clues or something."

Yvonne sniffed at my cursing. "There has to be something connecting us together," she said, her nasal voice grating on my nerves. "Where did you go to school again, Jane?"

My head pounded and, if I didn't get some water soon, I was going to murder them both.

Okay, okay, not really. I wasn't actually a murderer.

Something rippled through my memories again. That light and bits of glitter flying past me. I tried to hang on, to see what other images were linked to this one, but like before, it disappeared.

After this, I was going straight to urgent care so they could test me for all the things docs tested people for. Maybe I'd been dropped on my head and had a concussion.

Footsteps ran by the door, a little pitter-patter of soles on wood. The door creaked open, and I turned. Someone was here! Someone could help.

The lights went out.

Yvonne screamed.

"I got it, I got it, I got it," Michael said. He lit up his phone flashlight and pointed it at the empty doorway. Nothing. Just sharp shadows from furniture in the hallway. Pulling out my phone flashlight, I spun around the room, illuminating the abandoned furniture and the toys taking on terrifying characteristics in the shadowy light. Even the teddy bear lost in the corner on its side looked like it might suddenly come running at us, teeth bared. Sweat dripped down my spine, soaking my shirt.

Yvonne switched from screaming to letting out gulpy sobs, which was worse, somehow.

"What was that?" Michael asked.

I shook my head; my skin hummed so badly I felt like I couldn't walk straight. I didn't want to tell the others I could sense ghosts. I didn't even want to tell them there were ghosts around at all.

"We need to check the hallway," he whispered.

"Sounds good," I said. "Go do it."

"No fucking way, Jane."

Yvonne let out a wail loud enough to echo before sitting hard on the ground.

"Come on," Michael said. "You're braver than me."

"Fine," I said, stepping over Yvonne's splayed legs. Moving quickly, I peeked out of the doorway into the hallway, shining my phone flashlight into the darkness. Nothing moved, and from what I could see, doorways stretched into the darkness.

"There's nothing there," I said. "Probably just our imagination." Michael had joined Yvonne on the floor and was rubbing her back. The lights clicked back on, and he let out a yell. The nursery went from being terrifying to just spooky, but the humming in my skin and skull kept increasing. It felt like my teeth fillings were going to vibrate out of my head.

"Okay," I said, putting my hands on my hips and staring down at them. "We can either stay here, or we can find a way out."

"Here," Yvonne said, rocking back and forth.

"Really?" I said. "We'll die of hunger and thirst if we don't get out of this house. Michael?"

He gave Yvonne's back another rub. "I think we need to explore," he said, his voice gentle. "But I'm not letting Jane go by herself—"

Misogynistic asshole, I thought, but was wise enough not to say out loud.

"And we need you to come with us," he continued to Yvonne. "We can't leave you alone."

"I can't, I can't, I can't," she sobbed.

"The lights are on for the moment," I said. "We don't know how long that's going to last. You wanna be stuck in here by yourself with no lights? Don't be ridiculous."

Yvonne didn't respond.

"Chop, chop." I clapped my hands together.

"Come on, Jane's right." Michael stood up, pulling Yvonne to her feet. They were both covered with dust and grit from the floor. "Good job," he told Yvonne, like he'd say to a child.

I fought the urge to roll my eyes. The humming against my skin was getting worse, a sure sign there'd be some ghost activity, some voices, maybe even some objects moving. If I had my equipment, we'd probably have collected a couple of EVPs, voices recorded that we'd hear upon playback, and maybe have seen some movement in a heat sensitive camera. But with none of that, I just had my instincts screaming at me. This house was more than just a weird prank or game. Someone had trapped us in a severely haunted house for some unknown reason.

I stepped out into the hallway, no longer caring if Yvonne and Michael followed. I could see three doorways to my left, one to my right. A table with rotted flowers in a vase was directly across from our doorway and faded portraits lined the walls.

I looked down and had to take a deep breath. There were footprints out here, in the dust and dirt. Different sizes, but all with the tread of sneakers. It reminded me of the ghost hunting teams when we explored super abandoned places. We always left a ton of footprints with those interlocked sneaker treads.

Well, it was a good sign that someone knew about this place; especially with fresh tracks. If they got out, we could too. I darted back into the nursery and picked up a wooden bat. It was small, a child's weight, but I still took a practice swing. I could hurt someone with this if I needed to.

Not that I wanted to. Again, that memory tugged; the burst of light, a face coming out of the darkness, eyes wide and mouth open in a—

Gone again.

Stifling a groan, I opened up the door to the left and made a note in my phone. This room was a bedroom, a giant bed with opened rotting curtains dominating the space. I paused in the doorway, the curtains shifting in the nonexistent wind.

Acting on memory, I asked, "If anyone is present, show a sign."

"Why would you—?" Knocking interrupted Michael, sounding like it was coming from inside the surrounding walls. Whispers surrounded us, the voices too quiet to distinguish between gender or age.

"Focus on the candle."

"They have to be here."

"Stop being an idiot. You're ruining my focus."

"Stop it, guys."

Michael looked around, his eyes huge and terrified.

"Yeah," I said. "This place is super haunted. Have you guys ever done a ghost hunt?"

Michael shook his head. "I've monitored camera feeds at the hospital, though. Seen plenty of ghosts there. I have lots of footage and this whole blog about the ghosts at the hospital."

"They let you do that?" I asked. "Your boss?"

"They don't know," he said with a quick wink. "I get paid shit, and the ad revenue helps."

Guess he wasn't a pharmaceutical rep.

"You?" I asked Yvonne. "Anything you know about ghosts?"

She winced. "Under a pen name, I've written books about ghost hunts. True ghost stories… but… they were fake."

I nodded. "Most true ghost stories never actually happened. Ever gone on one of those ghost tours? Totally made up. But that's what ties us together. Ghosts."

A memory rippled again, but different. A bunch of people sitting around a ouija board, their faces lit by candles. But my angle was weird; like I was looking down on them.

Then the memory was gone, before I could really remember it. What was wrong with me? I didn't have memory problems. I always remembered my dreams. Though this was probably something out of a movie or a dream. I'd never touched a ouija board; I was too scared of what would happen.

"Okay," I said. "The fact we're trapped in a haunted house changes nothing. We still need to find a way out. That's our priority."

A voice called out of the darkness, surrounding us somehow, "Is anyone there? Make a sound if you're here." It was a young girl's voice, shaking a bit.

"Yes!" Yvonne shouted. "We're here!" She looked wildly around the rotting bedroom while Michael ran out into the hallway. "Anyone?" he called.

"We're up here," Yvonne called. "We're trapped!"

"Help us, please," Michael yelled.

The humming in my skin was becoming unbearable; my hands and feet shaking with the vibration. Something was coming.

The walls rang with knocks again and Yvonne shrieked, collapsing onto the floor, her hands over her ears. Michael let out a sob and sat down next to her, trying to calm her.

"Make it stop," he said, looking up at me, a tear running down his cheek.

I spun in circles. Where was this coming from?

Then everything stopped, like someone had thrown a switch. My ears rang. The room seemed lighter, more natural. Even the humming went away, and I let out my own groan.

Yvonne wailed.

"Let's get out of here," I said, grabbing one of her elbows and trying to get her to stand. "Michael, help me."

Between the two of us, we got Yvonne up, shuffling her out of the room and into the hallway. She leaned heavily on Michael, sobbing, snot running from her nose.

"I just want to go home," she moaned.

"I know," I said. "We're trying, but we need to keep moving. Maybe keep her out here with you," I told Michael, "while I check the rooms?"

"But you'll be alone." He wiped his nose on his shoulder, a giant snot streak left behind.

"But Yvonne needs you more." I managed not to roll my eyes. His misogynistic mind couldn't handle the idea that a woman might not need him.

"You can't explore on your own," he said. "If something happens to you, it'll break her."

Fine. "Ok, then while holding up Yvonne, maybe you can just lean in the doorway in each room and make sure nothing happens to me?"

His eyes were wide when he said, "I guess."

๑

An hour later, we'd mapped out most of the house, Yvonne stumbling from room to room, supported by Michael. The upstairs was actually pretty small, with four vast bedrooms, the nursery, and a gigantic bathroom with a chain pull toilet. I'd found a staircase to an attic behind one doorway and, while Michael stayed in the hall with Yvonne, I'd climbed the claustrophobic stairs, sure I was going to be attacked either from above or behind. But all I'd found was a shadowy room, full of dust motes, crates and rounded trunks.

Now we were mostly through the downstairs, the rooms connected oddly to each other without a centralized hallway or corridor. So far, we'd found the library, a kitchen, a dining room, and what I could only describe as a parlor room, full of formerly white furniture. I carefully noted all the rooms in my phone, trying to draw out a map we could reference again if needed to.

The only thing we hadn't found was a way out. All the windows were boarded to the point we couldn't tell if it was day or night. We hadn't heard any more voices or knocking, which was good, because I didn't think Yvonne would survive another scare.

I opened the next door, my foot hitting a pool ball. This was a game or billiard room. The pool table had rotted in a corner, releasing the balls for us to trip over. My skin hummed so violently in this room, I scratched at my arms. Out of the corner of my eye, something flitted, something with long dark hair caught into a bun on the top of their head.

I said nothing to the other two. Yvonne could barely walk, even with Michael's help, and she stank of urine.

We tried the windows and opened up any closed doors, just like we had the other room. But like the others, the windows were boarded up. Broken furniture like table legs, framed pictures, and even books had been nailed or screwed across the openings. As I'd done in every room, I tried to yank something off the window, but whoever had nailed and screwed the furniture into the window frames had done it so well, the bits of junk didn't even wiggle. I inspected three nails hammered in, almost on top of each other. Or maybe they'd been insane.

Michael helped Yvonne onto a barstool and picked up a pool cue. He stabbed it into the portrait covering a window, trying to gouge through the canvas. When it ripped, I helped him pull the art apart, but underneath was more wood.

"Is there even a window under here?" he grunted.

I looked at the window frame. "Maybe not. Maybe the glass is gone."

He slammed his fist against the wood and winced as his knuckles bled against it.

"Goddamn it," he said, sucking on his knuckles. "Goddamn it!" he screamed into the darkness.

Yvonne giggled, and I jumped at the sound. "This is crazy," she said. "Let us out!" she screamed. "Somebody, anybody!"

Whispers suddenly surrounded us, increasing and decreasing in volume.

"Did you hear that?"

"Ask again!"

"Guys, make it stop! This is too scary!"

Yvonne sobbed, covering up the sound of the whispers.

"Quiet," I said, trying to focus. The shadow flitted again, coming into the pool room from the parlor and disappearing into thin air as I stared at it. The whispers fizzled out, only to be replaced by the sound of footsteps on the stairs.

"Oh thank God," Yvonne said, running out of the room toward the staircase.

"No, wait," I yelled, sprinting after her. "Yvonne, come back!"

Michael and I caught up to her just as she was trying to hurry up the stairs. The footsteps continued, coming toward us, measured and loud enough to echo. As I watched, a shadow formed, someone walking down the stairs, a girl with her hair in a top bun. She held her arms out in front of her oddly.

Yvonne screamed, and the shadow spun before disappearing. Michael grabbed Yvonne, and she buried herself in his shirt. "I want out of here," she moaned.

"I know, I know," he murmured. "Can't you do anything, Jane?" he snapped at me.

"What would you like me to do?" I snapped back, hands on my hips. "We can't find any way out."

"There has to be something."

The girl-shaped shadow reappeared and resumed its slow progress down the stairs. But now more shadows appeared behind her, hurrying past us. I could almost see hands on the banisters grasping as the people raced down the stairs. It would be fascinating if it wasn't terrifying.

We moved out of the way of the shadows, and without stopping, they disappeared through the front door, like the boarded-up wood didn't exist.

Michael turned to me, his eyes wide and bloodshot. Yvonne sobbed, her face hidden in his shirt.

"What was that?" he asked.

"Ghosts," I said. "I think we scared them."

"Can't be more scared than I am," Michael said.

I put my hands on my hips. Whoever had locked us in here had needed a way out, or had just boarded up the windows and doors. One of the windows or doorways had to be something we could get through.

"We need to go over it again," I said. "Start upstairs and look around again. We're missing something."

"No," Michael said. "We're going to go into this room," he pointed at the parlor with its dusty white furniture. "And we're just going to wait until morning. Until someone comes and gets us."

He led Yvonne into the room, helping her sit on a couch. She curled up into herself, lying down and wrapping her arms around her knees in some sort of bizarre fetal position. Michael pulled me aside. "We need to get out of here," he said.

"Cool," I said. "When I just said that, you said that we were going to wait until morning. Can't have it both ways." We turned back to Yvonne, but she was gone.

She was gone.

She Was Gone.

SHE WAS GONE.

I gasped just as Michael shouted. Racing over to the couch, we looked behind and under it. Nothing.

"Yvonne," I shouted, then stopped as it seemed to echo throughout the house. A scream sounded, then a giggle. I didn't realize I could get more scared, but I felt my bladder loosen.

"I'm getting out of here," Michael said. He raced to the door, banging on it, flinging himself against it. A shadow flitted across my field of vision and I turned to look. A girl stared back at me, pointing what looked like a tiny camera at us.

"Help us," I begged her. "Help us get out of here."

But she just panned the camera back and forth. "I thought I saw something," she called back. "But—" and then she disappeared.

Wait a minute.

Michael kept flinging himself at the door, scratches gouging his hands. I pulled him away.

"Stop," I said. "Stop it now."

"We need to get out!"

"We can't!" I shouted. "Shut up for a minute and let me think."

Ghosts existed out of sync with the living. The spaces they see are different than the ones we see. That's why ghosts appear and disappear and seem to walk through doorways. The beings, the teenagers we were seeing, appeared and disappeared. Yvonne had disappeared. I thought back to the ripples of memories I'd kept having.

"Do you remember a bright light?" I asked Michael. "Coming at you?"

He shook his head and held out his hands. The scratches were gone. "Where'd my scratches go?" he demanded. "Why don't my hands hurt?"

My knees buckled. There were ghosts here, but it wasn't the teenagers we kept seeing.

"Seriously," I said. "Think back. The bright light." I tried to remember. A car engine sounding. Brakes squealing. A punch in my stomach, being weightless.

"Do you remember a car?"

He shook his head, then paused. "Wait a minute. I remember coming out from the restaurant." He tugged at his lip. "I remember people screaming. I remember…" He touched his stomach. "The car hit me." He dug his hands into my arms, shaking me. "The car hit me, and I don't remember what happened after that!"

"Okay," I said, taking a deep breath. How had we gotten here? What had the whispers been saying? There'd been something about a candle, and I'd seen a ouija board. And I'd seen people on the stairs, carrying what looked like a camera.

"Oh my God," I whispered. "We're dead. We're the ghosts."

"What?" Michael demanded.

"I think we were part of a seance. They must have used a ouija board here, in this abandoned place." I looked at the boarded-up windows and doors. "I think they called us up. I think they trapped us here."

We would never get out.

CHAPTER 6
CIGARS AND CRITTERS

I UNLACED MY BOOTS, putting my socked feet on my desk and leaning back, lighting a thick black cigar. The dark smoke circled around my head and I breathed out, feeling the drug enter my system. Things blurred slightly.

It was a celebratory cigar, a celebratory moment of relaxation. Our festival had made a ship-full of money from the farmers and colonists on New Tenali. It hadn't seemed like a thriving community when we'd landed, but the farmers had spent more than we'd expected; they must not get many travelers. They'd loved our critters from defunct portal planets. I remembered the women, their hair in practical braids, petting the horses from Dead Earth while men in their muddy boots pointed at the birds with black and white scales from Dead Belem and the kids with calloused hands from farming dared each other to touch the sparkling and dangerous rainbow fish from Dead Red Yen.

My eyes closed, my thoughts liquifying, my body sinking into the padded chair while the sounds of my ship faded into the darkness.

"Captain?"

I nearly jumped out of my chair, but controlled the

instinct. Though I probably twitched. My second in command, Sam, loved sneaking into my private quarters when I wanted to be left alone. Short and skinny, sometimes I wondered if he oozed between the bulkheads, appearing wherever he wanted. I didn't want to give him the satisfaction of startling me.

Wow, this cigar was strong. I shook away the nasty thought.

"What'd you want?" I asked, keeping my eyes closed. and my body relaxed. "Didn't I put you in charge so I wouldn't be bugged?" The cigar was making me mean, but all I wanted was a few hours off. It had been a pretty good day, and I wanted to enjoy some time alone.

"We have a problem. We can't take off."

My heart sunk, though I kept my eyes closed. Sam never exaggerated.

"Why?"

"The villagers won't let us leave."

"What'd you mean, 'won't let us leave'? We're in a bloody spaceship. They can't stop us." I sat up and snubbed out the cigar in its ashtray. "We need to hit New Moores in ten days and not a moment later so we can set up all the critters at their… what'd they call it? Inspiration Point? Or we have to refund the deposit. And there's no com signal this far out to tell them we'd be late. We need to leave now."

"They say the transport ships aren't coming. They want us to take as many of them as we can with us. They want us to take the children."

My heart dropped into my stomach. "The townfolk here shouldn't need transport ships yet, right? Unless they've been using portal technology, their planet should be fine." The air had been breathable, though a bit sulphury. I hadn't noticed any signs of planet decay, the storms, the earthquakes, the animal migrations, the plant death, or the oxygen tanks humans on decaying planets needed. But I hadn't been looking either; I'd been running a festival, a celebration of food and drink, arts and animals from dead planets.

I pressed a button on my wrist unit, waking my scientist and third in command. "Riggs."

"Wha— "

"How long does New Tajito have?"

"Wha—" Riggs was a pain to wake up. I could just imagine him sitting up in bed, rubbing his eyes and stretching out a kink in his neck. And in my thoughts, he wasn't wearing anything, his muscles rippling across his chest.

I shook my head, clearing the image. Stupid cigar. I shouldn't have smoked it.

"New Tajito," I repeated. "The planet we're on. How much time does it have?"

"A few weeks, according to the readings I took." His voice echoed slightly across the com. "I figured the villagers didn't want to leave. That's why we had such a good festival. They knew they'd all die soon when their planet decayed. Though they do seem like the type who would all commit suicide in some sort of ritual."

I rounded on Sam. "We're on a planet that's going to decay in a few weeks?"

Sam's eyebrows twitched, his only sign of embarrassment. "We missed the warnings. That was my fault."

"No one should be on this planet. It's not safe. An earthquake or a storm could've trapped us here!"

Over five hundred years ago, scientists figured out how to create portals into different worlds. Humans, being what we are, especially on a planet dying of overuse and squabbles over the fixes, spread out across the universe, stepping onto planets we didn't belong on. It was chaos. Some emigrated to set up new societies, those societies based on religion, philosophy, or on the rules of the Australian Outback back when it was a penal colony. Thousands died stepping onto worlds they didn't belong, and millions of various animals and plant life died or became extinct as humans brought them back and forth through portals.

Instead of learning from my destroyed planet, we started on others, ruining land, flora and fauna and spreading like a plague. We mined planets for various minerals and gems we didn't have. We scarred planets, uprooting plant life, hunting animals and building structures that may or may not have used natural resources. We introduced predators and prey to planets that had none. We destroyed hundreds of worlds, over the course of a few years, only thinking of what we wanted; whether it was money, a new life, or new adventures.

But it was the portal technology itself that caused the most damage, literally destabilizing the atmosphere of the planets. Earth was the first to go, all the animals and plants dying as extreme weather and oxygen depletion wreaked havoc. Governments outlawed portal technology, with steep consequences for its use, but the technology thrived on the black market, and it was easy to get between worlds. Knowing our planet had no time, the last of the governments and scientists banded together and funded space travel, creating ships, and space stations we could live on. We pushed out into the galaxy, eventually finding the worlds the portals connected to.

Tourist trade developed and ships like ours committed to not using portal technology carried art, music, animals, and colonists back and forth. My ship, the Miscellany, made its money setting up festivals similar to circuses on Dead Earth. Of course, portal technology continued, the ease of transportation trumping the longevity of space travel. And planets continued to decay.

"Captain," Riggs' voice melted through my unit, bringing me back to reality. "Did you need me? Or can I go back to sleep?"

"Meet us in the storage bay." I clicked off the unit and turned to Sam. "Go tell—" My thoughts wandered away. I grabbed a full water container and drained it. I had to get the drug out of my system so I could think.

"What planet are we close to?"

"New Akeno is five days out."

"Go tell them to get some transports out here. Even if we have to pay for them."

"They're not in com range. No one is in com range."

Duh. Stupid cigar.

"That's why they couldn't ask for help," I muttered. "Doesn't this planet have some sort of a central leader? And not that weird mayor we met."

"Gone. These are the people that's left."

For just a second, my shoulders sagged. No wonder the villagers had spent so well on our candies, pastries, and alcohol-laced drinks. Some had paid multiple times to stare at the caged critters and the ancient art. They knew they were going to die.

Something hit the outside of the ship. "What the bloody hell?"

"They're rioting," Sam said. "They think we won't take off if they climb onto the outside of the ship,"

"If all of them climb on, they're right," I said. I put my boots on, relacing them up to my knees and quickly re-braiding my long dark hair, glad I hadn't bothered to change into more comfortable clothes. "What the hell are they thinking? If we can't take off, we all die, including them. Bloody village idiots."

"They'll let us take off if we agree to their terms," Sam said.

"Course they will," I muttered.

Together, we went down the narrow stairwells to the storage bay. I liked money, but enjoyed spending it more, so everything in Miscellany was updated, clean and fresh. Our hallways had tile floors, soft gray paint, and art from dead planets. Every so often, we passed a communal area full of soft couches, chairs, and pillows. I used most of our crew for the critters and festivals, so they had lots of downtime and I wanted them comfortable and happy.

It cut down on problems.

We finally reached the storage bay. The bay doors were open to the starlight and the mob mutterings. My crew moved crates that hooted, hissed, and growled inside the ship. They worked to calm the horses racing around their paddock, hoofs clanging against the metal, foam dripping, panicking from the mob noises. Outside, the villagers were a dark mass of moving torches and flashlights. Between the flickering light and moonlight from the two moons, there seemed to be more than five hundred. Two of my security stood at the entrance, their guns out, keeping people back.

"Riggs," I yelled.

"Here," he said, coming up behind me and zipping up a sweatshirt. I didn't force my crew to wear uniforms, and he wore dark pants in addition to his sweatshirt. His cheek still had pillow lines and his brown hair lay flat against his head.

God, I'd give anything to see him like that every morning.

Almost.

I approached the mob and nodded at my security. They stepped back, and I waited, my arms folded, back-lit by the ship's lights, Riggs on my right and Sam on my left.

The crowd quieted, and the man I'd thought was the mayor approached us.

"Captain. Ma'am. Please. We have children. Please take them. With you."

My insides froze, just for a second.

I took a deep breath. "We can't." I kept my tone flat and clipped. "Our ship is carefully balanced. Too much water and carbon dioxide in the air and the ship won't make fuel correctly. If we don't have fuel, we can't fly."

The crowd whispered my words, echoing them to the

people in the back. Then they roared, shouting things at me, demanding I prevent their extinction.

Riggs put a hand on my shoulder and leaned forward. "We can take five kids, max," he breathed into my ear, his lips making tingles run down my neck and back. My pulse sped up. I had to get that cigar out of my system.

"What would we do with them?" I breathed back, loud enough for Sam to hear. "They can't stay with us. We'd have to drop them off on another planet, and they'd end up in a slave market within a week."

Sam nodded once, agreeing with me.

"We can't take anyone," I answered the mob. "As soon as we get within com distance, I'll hire a transport ship for you." And I would, knowing there was no way the villagers could pay me back, even if they hadn't spent all their money at my festival. I had a Picasso I could sell that would cover the cost.

In the distance, lightning flashed, and the earth shook, the sulfur smell increasing. A few coughed, and I saw them fumble in their pockets, attaching tiny plastic hoses to their noses. How had we missed this?

"Captain," Riggs muttered behind me. "We can help a little."

"We can't," Sam said, his lips barely moving. "It'll be death for them. Just at a different place and time."

"Every time we fly, we risk death," Riggs said. "We really can't try?"

I glanced at him, and he held my eyes with his.

"Please Jess," he whispered.

I looked at Sam. He never let emotion help guide his decisions. I didn't like him, but he was the best second in command I'd ever had. He wouldn't allow this. I could make him the bad guy, at least. Make Riggs hate him instead of me.

"Five?" Sam asked.

"It'll be tight, but yes," Riggs said. "We'll need to ration water and food, but we can do it."

Sam looked out at the crowd, and his lips pulled down on the corners. He nodded once.

This was a mistake.

"Fine," I said to the mayor. "We'll take five. I don't know how you're going to choose, but with the storm coming, you'll have to—"

"We already chose." Five kids stepped forward, bags over their shoulders. At least twenty more, each with their own bag stepped back into the crowd.

Ice coiled in my belly and flew up to my heart.

I breathed once, raised my chin and nodded toward the five. I turned my back as they said goodbye to their families.

"Pack it in," I said to the rest of my crew. "Quickly. Before the villagers storm the ship and demand we take more children."

Bags and boxes were shifted, the critters moved back to their enclosures. I held out my hand to a horse, and it trotted over, hoping for the fake sugar cubes I often fed them. I rubbed its velvety nose, pushing the ice in my chest back down, until I could breathe.

"Captain," Riggs breathed behind me.

I turned to my new passengers: three girls, two boys, dressed in layered clothes. They were in their early teens—young enough to need saving, but old enough to work and protect themselves if necessary. All wore pants and boots with jackets, scarves, and working gloves. The girls' hair was pulled back from their face and the boys looked strong. I bet their packs had food, water, a small weapon, some money, and no sentimental items. Their parents had prepared them for an unclear future the only way they knew how.

They met my eyes, nodding at me, though one girl had a tear running down her cheek. They didn't look back on their home as we closed the storage bay doors. I put my hands behind my back so they wouldn't see them shake.

I introduced Riggs and Sam and explained my rules. Do

what you're told, stay in your bunks or the common areas, do not go near the critters without permission, if you see something odd, alert the crew. "We'll be rationing for the next ten days, so if you have food and water, please turn it into the galley." I pointed at one of the security guards and told them to give the kids a tour.

"We'll hire a transport ship as soon as we're within range," I said. "We'll try to get the rest of your village off the planet. And we'll drop you off on New Moores in about ten days when we get there."

They nodded, and I watched them walk away to the guest bunks. They'd have to double and triple up, but that wasn't my problem.

Wait, I was the captain. Of course, it was my problem.

"You're in charge," I said to Sam. "I'll relieve you in six hours. I need sleep. Riggs, make sure you set our waste balances. We don't want to run out of fuel because there's too much carbon dioxide in the system."

"Yes, Captain," Sam said, walking off.

"Jess," Riggs whispered. I didn't look at him; my crew was still putting crates away, unrolling the grass for the horses, and folding up festival enclosures. A red bird, a cardy, flapped over our heads, and someone cursed.

"Just get the balances right," I said.

"Jess," he said under his breath. "Thank you." He touched my arm, a quick contact I hoped no one saw. My skin tingled, and I closed my eyes, memorizing the moment.

I glanced up at him, and he gave me a half smile that didn't reach his eyes. God, I was in an idiot, high on some stupid drug I shouldn't have taken, good day or not.

And today was not a good day.

My com went off an hour later. I wasn't asleep, but lying in the partial darkness, wishing my brain would stop chattering. It'd only gotten worse as the drug left my system.

Five hundred people, a dead planet and no transports. And we could only take five. There had to be something we could do.

I pushed the button.

"We have a problem," Sam said. "And could use you on the bridge."

I laced up my jacket and pulled on my boots. I'd released my hair out of its braid when I'd laid down and I tried to smooth it and twist it back up as I climbed the ladder to the bridge.

Maybe our guests had staged a mutiny. Maybe they would kill us all. Maybe this was all a trap.

My bridge gleamed with the latest navigation and ship running systems. It was tiny but functional. We didn't need much to run the ship, but the three of us each had our own seats with our own screens.

I sat down, and a chime sounded. I looked at my display —there were too many blinking red bars.

"Our balance is off, and we're almost out of fuel," Riggs said. "We'll be dead in the water in about three hours, and we don't have enough to make it back to New Tajito."

Ah. That explained the red lights.

"Five children was too many?" Sam rumbled.

Riggs shook his head, his hair standing up on end from tugging on it. "I went over and over it. Five is fine."

"Something malfunctioning?" I asked.

He shook his head again. "I checked. There'd be alarms."

I raised an eyebrow.

"More alarms," he clarified. "Different alarms."

"Get the engineer, and go over it again," I said to Riggs.

"It's almost like someone is breathing more than they should," Riggs muttered. "Or we took on more than five."

Bloody hell.

"We have stowaways," I said with a sigh.

Sam's lips twisted. "Should've expected this."

"Yep," I said. "They were desperate and let us go without argument. Sam, get security to search the ship. Riggs, double check, be sure we don't have a leak somewhere."

Sam reported back an hour later. They'd found six additional children and a baby. We wouldn't make it to New Moores.

Four hours later, we still moved, barely. We'd jerry-rigged our fuel system, but it hadn't helped. Now we'd resorted to firing our blasters in small puffs, so we headed toward the closest shipping lane, four days out. We'd set up an emergency hail on repeat, but no one had answered. New Tajito really was in the middle of nowhere.

I'd told everyone to stop breathing, but they weren't listening.

"We just need to get to a shipping lane," I said for the hundredth time. "We can message for help. Get a tow. It'll cost us, but it's better than bloody dying out here in space."

"We're trying, Captain," Riggs said for probably the hundredth time.

I couldn't believe my security team had allowed six extra kids to sneak on board. As soon as we got to a planet, I was going to kick them off my ship and then off the bloody planet itself.

"We have to kill them," Sam said.

"No," I answered.

"But they're putting out the most carbon dioxide, other than the humans."

"The horses are our livelihood," I said. "And no one else has them."

"It's that or dying," Sam said.

"Fine," I snapped to Riggs and then regretted it. "Do the calculations, please."

Riggs nodded, the corner of his mouth twitching in a quick half smile for me, letting me know he wasn't taking offense.

"Captain," Sam said. "A ship is within hailing distance."

I glanced at the display. "Junker," I sneered. Junkers scavenged abandoned ships taking whatever they could. They also went down to planets near decay, gathering anything that remained. Accidents and genetic mutations were common among the crew. And most were slave traders. Though they condemned the use of portal technology, so that was a plus at least.

"Captain," Sam said. "They'll take the kids."

"No," Riggs said.

"If we reduce our population by five, we can make it to New Moores," Sam said.

"Absolutely not," I said.

"We can keep the baby, at least."

"No."

"Captain, it's an option," Sam said. "It's that or we all die."

"Sam, I forbid you to say, we're-all-going-to-die-if-we-don't-do-what-you-want. Riggs and I know we'll die if we don't figure this out."

Sam's gaze hardened, which I hadn't thought was possible.

"If there's one ship, they'll be more," I said. "Riggs, how closer to the lane will we get if we kill the horses?"

"Maybe a day. But the further off our balances get, the harder it'll be to produce fuel and it's hard to calculate. We've never had this many breathing things on board."

We had to get to New Moores or a shipping lane. The baby had come on board with a week of formula one kid had already spilled. She wouldn't survive on the evaporated milk we had in the pantry.

"Is there some sort of equipment to help balance our CO2

and fuel levels?" I asked. "Something the junker ship would have?"

Riggs and Sam stared at each other. "What about InferiorHYP Tube?" Sam asked.

Riggs shrugged. "If they have the right size, it could help."

"Fine." I pressed the com button. "This is Miscellany calling Rusty Bullet." I flicked the mute button. "Is that seriously their name?" I asked Sam and Riggs. They ignored me, which was probably best.

"This is Rusty Bullet responding." The male voice was deep and tired. "You seem dead in the water. Need help?"

"Naw," I answered. "Our balances got a little off. Picked up some stowaways. Just waiting for things to come to alignment. Whatever you do, don't go to New Tajito. Transport ships never came, and the population is desperate."

"Hence the stowaways. You're not the first. Why'd you go there? That's been a no fly for a month."

I gave Sam a dirty look, which he ignored.

"We're a traveling festival and show unique items from all over the galaxy." I said. I sent them our promo clip. Let them think we were a bunch of imbeciles that couldn't fly a ship.

"Guess it takes all kinds," the voice said.

"It does. Do you happen to have an InferiorHYP tube? We're going to be fine, but that would speed things up."

"I just might. You got someone that can install it?"

"Of course. How much?" This was going to cost us everything. They knew we needed the tube.

"Here's the thing, captain,"

Oh jeez. Here we go.

"Yep?"

There was a pause on the line. "We need a doctor. And with thirty-three people on board, even if some of them are stowaways, you would have a doctor."

"Sorry, we don't have one," I said. "We can trade, though.

I have art and valuable cargo, for example."

Riggs raised his eyebrow at me. Okay, he was technically our doctor and could treat things like a doctor could. We just never needed him for that. We'd been lucky, I realized.

"Then we can't sell you our InferiorHYP Tube." The voice on the other end sounded defeated, not triumphant.

"Then we all die," I said.

"We?"

"If you're willing to trade for a doctor, you're in pretty awful shape." I ignored Riggs, pointing and mouthing something. If I didn't look, I didn't have to notice.

"We were already dead," the voice said. "You had a chance."

Riggs reached across the com. "This is Science Officer Thomas Riggs. What's going on that you need a doctor? We have some supplies we can trade."

"Negative. It's Iverson disease."

Ship sickness. It was preventable with good sanitation, but difficult to get rid of. And it could wipe out half the crew, even with treatment. They truly needed a doctor, or they'd die.

Why was everyone I met lately close to death?

"We have supplies that can help," I said. "But no doctor."

"We have plenty of supplies," the voice answered. "We don't know how to use them."

"Then you'll die," I said.

"So will you."

I was going to scream. Couldn't anything go right today?

"Jess," Riggs said softly.

No. "Where there's one ship, they'll be more," I said to Riggs and Sam. "We let them go."

"I can help," Riggs said.

"No."

"They will die," he said. "I can save us and them."

But…

"Jess, it's okay."

The door to the bridge snicked open and closed. Sam had stepped out.

I took a deep breath. "We can't lose you. You're our third in command. There's another way. If we kill the horses, we can make it close to a shipping lane. There'll be other ships. And I would murder Sam without you."

He took my hand, raised it to his lips, and kissed it. We'd never touched each other, we'd done nothing. Why had we made that decision? It seemed stupid now.

"Tom," I whispered. He stepped closer and stroked a loose strand of hair, then traced his hand from my ear along my jaw. He stared at me, like he was memorizing me. I closed my eyes, and he leaned his forehead against mine. Why hadn't we taken the time before?

"When I see you again, you won't be my captain," he said. He smiled and this time it reached his eyes.

"Three months," I said and named a city and planet light years away. "I'll be there waiting for you in three months." It was a strong planet with harsh laws for those caught with portal technology. It wouldn't decay any time soon.

"It's a promise," he said.

We both knew he was lying—he'd probably contract Iverson disease and die. Plus, it wasn't like Rusty Bullet would just let him go.

But it was something.

He touched his lips to mine, one kiss, sweet and intense and more than I'd ever hoped for. He tasted of mint and spring and lazy weekends spent in bed. He tasted of a future I wanted.

We pulled apart, and I touched the com. "We can give you our doctor in exchange for the InferiorHYP Tube."

"Excellent," the voice on the other side said.

Riggs held my hand, kissing it again.

Three months wasn't that long. I could survive this.

AUTHORS NOTE

I have a confession to make. I've always wanted to step through a portal into another world. I think most writers do; that's why we write. But I've always had an affection for portal worlds like Oz and Narnia. I've always wondered what happens to those that fall into those portals and those that make it back out. There's a choice you make when you step through a portal, and things you gain and things you lose. Does what you lose make up for what you gain? And who are these lucky, or unlucky ones that get to step through doorways, gateways and portals?

Anyways, this collection is my exploration of this. I've already had multiple requests from my editors and beta readers to explore some of these worlds further and that's definitely on the horizon. Along with all my other ideas.

I'd like to thank M.S. Ewing, Stephanie Reali and Morrigan Puhr for being early beta readers, telling me two of my stories didn't really work, and forcing me to rewrite them. I'd also like to thank the fabulous Chris Bannor who edited Tiny Gateways for me, and made these stories so much more than they could've been without her. I'd also like to thank S.

Faxon for her beautiful cover, formatting help and business acumen. We're getting there in this world!

My parents were the first to introduce me to the world of Oz, the first place I couldn't wait to visit, if only I wished hard enough. Thank you for opening the door to a joy of reading and a lifetime of imaginings.

And finally, as always, my family for giving me the time and space to pursue this dream. And to my husband, who puts up with my editing during car rides, demanding places to charge my laptop in airports (for more editing) and who will listen to my ramblings about plot and characters–thank you for everything!

Please leave a review

If you enjoyed this collection of short stories, please leave a review on the site you purchased it on and/or on Goodreads. Not only do reviews give authors a chance to improve their storytelling, but it's vital for the success of our business.

Thank you and I hope you enjoyed this collection of short stories.

ALSO BY THERESA HALVORSEN

Warehouse Dreams

River City Widows

Lost Aboard

How to Be A Successful Author and Not Lose Your Mind

ABOUT THE AUTHOR

Theresa Halvorsen has never met a profanity she hasn't enjoyed. She's generally overly-caffeinated and at times, wine-soaked. The author of multiple spec-fiction works, including Warehouse Dreams, Lost Aboard and River City Widows, besides various short stories and non-fiction articles, Theresa wonders what sleep is. Because she didn't have enough to do, she also started No Bad Books Press with S. Faxon, and edits for other spec-fiction writers. When she's not writing, editing, publishing or podcasting with the Semi-Sages of the Pages, she's commuting through San Diego traffic to her healthcare position. In whatever free time is left (ha!), Theresa enjoys board games, geeky conventions, and reading. Her life goal is to give "Oh-My-Gosh-This-Book-Is-So-Good!" happiness to her readers. She lives in Temecula with her amazing husband, occasionally her college-age twins, and the pets they'd promised to care for. Find her at www.theresaHauthor.com and on Tiktok and Facebook.